Red Peru

"Just a minute," Stantington began.

"We may not have a minute, thanks to your bumbling," Smith said. "Did the President authorize closing down Project Omega?"

"Not exactly," the CIA chief said.

"Weren't you aware that there is a notation in the CIA's permanent records that Project Omega can be closed down only on the specific written authorization of the President of the United States?"

"Never mind that," Stantington replied. "Since it's been closed down, two Russian diplomats have been killed. The Russians are blaming it on us. They say that both assassins were on our payroll."

"That's right," said Smith. "They were." He spun around in his chair and looked out the one-way windows. "And that's not the worst of it. The Russian premier is on the hit list, too."

"Oh, my god," Stantington said. He slumped back in the couch. "How can we stop it?"

Smith turned back. His face still showed no emotion.

"We can't," he said. "Once Project Omega has been set in motion, it can't be stopped."

THE DESTROYER SERIES

The Destroyer

LAST CALL #35

by Richard Sapir & Warren Murphy

PINNACLE BOOKS   LOS ANGELES

DESTROYER #35: LAST CALL

An original Pinnacle Books edition, published for the first time anywhere.

First printing, December 1978

ISBN: 0-523-40157-4

Cover illustration by Hector Garrido

Printed in the United States of America

PINNACLE BOOKS, INC.
2029 Century Park East
Los Angeles, California 90067

For Alice B.
in Boston

LAST CALL

CHAPTER ONE

It would have seemed like a crime against nature if Admiral Wingate Stantington (USN Retired) had not risen to a position of great prominence in the United States. The new head of the Central Intelligence Agency was the sturdy, clean-faced epitome of the best of all his schools. He had gotten his character from Annapolis, his computer efficiency from Harvard Business School, his culture from Oxford. He had been a Rhodes scholar and a second-string all-American halfback for the Navy.

His ice blue eyes twinkled with wit and strength, exuding a certain happy courage that had shown America over its television screens that brains and pluck and a new broom were now sweeping our intelligence agencies into a lean, clean top-flight group that not only America but the whole world could be proud of.

Sixty minutes before he was to make an off-hand decision that could trigger World War III, Admiral Stantington was arguing with a man who obviously had not read the *New York Times* Sunday magazine article about Stantington's ir-

1

resistible "he gets what he wants but always with a smile" charm.

"Shove it, Stantington," the man said. He was sitting in a hard-backed wooden chair in the middle of a bare room in a federal detention center outside Washington, D.C. The man wore light, plastic-framed, round eyeglasses that were too small for his face, the big sturdy round open face of an Iowa farmer.

Stantington walked in circles around the man, his tall, trim athletic body moving as briskly as if he were on a parade ground. He wore a light blue shadow-striped suit that accentuated his height and whose color went well with his eyes and his impeccably styled sandy hair with the faint touch of gray distinction over each temple.

"That's not really the tack to take," Stantington said in his soft Southern accent. "A little cooperation now might help you in the future."

The prisoner looked up at Stantington and his eyes narrowed behind the thick-lensed glasses.

"A little cooperation?" he said. "A little cooperation? You've got thirty-five years of my cooperation and what did I get for it? A jail sentence." He turned his face away and crossed his arms stubbornly, covering the printed number on his chest. He wore twill prisoner's fatigues.

Stantington walked around him again until he was in front of the prisoner and the man could see the new CIA director's winning smile.

"That's all water under the bridge," Stantington said. "Come on. Why don't you just tell me where it is?"

2

"Go to hell. You and that peckerhead you work for."

"Dammit, man. I want that key."

"Will you please tell me why a forty-nine-cent key is so important to you?" the prisoner asked.

"Because it is," Stantington said. He wanted to grab the man by the throat and wring the truth out of him. Or call in a CIA goon squad and have them apply electrodes to his testicles and shock the answer out of him. But there was no more of that. That was the old CIA, the discredited CIA, and it was probably knowing that the CIA *had* changed that made this prisoner so truculent and unreasonable.

"I threw it in a sewer so you couldn't get your manicured hands on it," the prisoner said. "No. No, I didn't. I had a hundred copies made and I gave them away to everybody and when you're not looking they're going to sneak into your office and go into your private bathroom and piss in your sink."

Admiral Wingate Stantington took a deep breath and clenched his hands behind his back.

"If that's the way you want it," he said to the prisoner. "But I just want you to know I won't forget this. If I have anything to say about it, you can kiss your pension goodbye. If I have anything to say about it, you'll serve out every goddamn last day of your term. And if I have anything to say about it, people like you will never again have anything to do with this country's intelligence apparatus."

"Go piss up a rope," the prisoner said.

Stantington walked briskly toward the door of

the bare room. His pedometer, which measured how many miles he walked each day, clicked against his right hip. At the door, the prisoner called his name. Stantington turned around and looked back into his eyes.

"It's going to happen to you too, Stantington," the man said. "Even as dumb as you are, you're going to try to do your best and one day they'll change the rules in the middle of the game and your ass'll be grass, just like mine. I'll save you a spot in the prison chow line."

And the former director of the Central Intelligence Agency smiled at Stantington, who walked out of the room without comment, a deep sense of disquiet and irritation flooding his mind.

Admiral Wingate Stantington brooded in the back of his limousine, all the way back to CIA headquarters in Langley, Virginia, just a few miles from Washington, D.C. He had wanted that key to the private bathroom in his office. *Time* magazine was coming the next week, probably to do a cover story on him, and he had already written the lead of the story in his mind:

Admiral Wingate Stantington, the man chosen to lead the beleagured Central Intelligence Agency, is both brilliant and budget-minded. In case anyone doubts that last point, when Stantington was installed in his new office last week, he found the door to his private washroom locked. The only key, he was told, was in the possession of the former director of the CIA, now serving a five-year jail term. Rather than call a locksmith and

4

put in a new lock ($23.65 by current Washington prices), Admiral Stantington drove by the prison on his way to work the next day and got the key from his predecessor. 'That's the way we're running things around here from now on,' Stantington said when he reluctantly confirmed the story. 'A tight ship is one that doesn't leak and that includes not leaking money,' he said."

To hell with it, Stantington thought. *Time* magazine would have to think of some other lead for its story. He couldn't be expected to do everybody's job for them.

The admiral was in his office at 9 A.M. He called his secretary on the intercom and told her to get a locksmith *tout de suite* and get a new lock for his bathroom door.

"And get two keys," he said. "And you keep one."

"Yes, sir," the young woman said, slightly surprised, because she hadn't thought it took a CIA command decision to get two keys for a new lock.

When he clicked off his intercom, Stantington checked his pedometer and found that he had already walked one and a half miles of his ten-mile daily quota. It gave him his first warm feeling of the day.

The second warm feeling came twenty minutes later when he met with his director of operations and chief of personnel and signed an order terminating the employment of 250 field agents and, thus, with a stroke of the pen, accomplishing the kind of decimation of the CIA's field forces that the Russians had lusted after for years but had always been unable to accomplish.

"Have to show them up on the Hill that we mean business," the CIA director said. "Anything else?"

He looked at the two men. His chief of operations, a round man who sweated a lot and had yellow teeth, said "Here's something you'll like, Admiral. It's called Project Omega and it's ours."

"I've never heard of it. What's its function?"

"That's just it. It doesn't have any function. The biggest damned no-show job I've ever seen." The operations director spoke in a crackly Southern accent. He was a lifelong friend of Stantington's and had formerly headed the highway system of a Southern state. He got the CIA job, out of a large group of other close political friends, because he was the only one who had never been indicted for taking construction kickbacks.

"They don't do a damn thing," the operations director said. "They sit around and play cards and the only thing even vaguely worklike they do is make a phone call once a day. Six agents. Nothing but one phone call a day."

Stantington was pacing the perimeter of his office, making neat 90-degree turns at each corner.

"Who do they call?" he asked.

"Somebody's aunt, I think. A little old lady in Atlanta."

"And their budget is how much?"

"Four million nine hundred thousand. But it's not all salaries of course. Some of it gets hard to trace."

Stantington whistled, a small sip of noise. "Four million nine hundred thousand," he said aloud. "Fire them. Imagine if *Time* magazine found that one out."

"*Time* magazine?" said the director of operations.

"Forget it," Stantington said.

"Should I check the old lady out?"

"No, dammit. Check her out and that'll cost money. Everything around here costs money. You can't even go to the toilet without it costing you twenty-three dollars and sixty-five cents. No. We check her out and that pushes the cost of this Omega whatever-it-is up to five million. And that's a bad number. Nobody's going to remember four million nine hundred thousand, but give them five million and they'll notice that. And then they'll start, five million here and ten million there and they'll nickel and dime us to death. Let that happen and we'll be crapping in the hallways."

The director of operations and the chief of personnel looked at each other quizzically. Neither understood the admiral's obsession with bathrooms, but both nodded at the Omega decision. The project, whatever it was, had no linkage to any program anywhere. The group was connected to nothing but the old lady in Atlanta and she was nothing. Without notifying anyone, the personnel director had checked. She was nothing and knew nothing or nobody. He had checked because he thought she might be related to the President. Everybody in that part of the country seemed to be. But she wasn't. It was agreed wholeheartedly. Fire them. Toss them overboard.

At 10 A.M., the six Project Omega agents were notified that they were separated from the service as of that minute.

None of them complained. None of them knew what he was supposed to be doing anyway.

Admiral Wingate Stantington continued to pace around his room when the two men left. He was composing a new lead for the *Time* cover story.

Between 9 and 9:20 A.M. last Tuesday morning, Admiral Wingate Stantington, the new director of the Central Intelligence Agency, fired 256 agents, saving America's taxpayers almost ten million dollars. It was just the start of a good day's work.

Not bad, Stantington thought. He smiled. It *was* just the start of a good day's work.

In a small frame house just off Paces Ferry Road on the outskirts of Atlanta, Mrs. Amelia Binkings stood at her kitchen sink, peeling apples with stiff arthritic fingers. She glanced at the clock over the sink. It was 10:54 A.M. Her telephone call would come in a minute. They came at different times each morning and she had a plastic laminated chart that told her what time to expect the call on each day. But after twenty years of getting the telephone calls, she had the chart memorized, so she'd put it in the closet under her good dishes. Ten fifty-five A.M. That's when the

8

call would come. There was no question about it, so she turned off the faucet and dried her hands on the ironed cotton towel she kept on a rack over the sink. She walked slowly over to the kitchen table and sat there, waiting for the phone to ring.

She had often wondered about the men who called her. Over the years she had gotten to recognize six separate voices. For a long time, she had tried to engage them in conversation. But they never said anything more than "Hi, honey. All's well." And then they hung up.

Sometimes she wondered if what she was doing was . . . well, was proper. It seemed like very little to do for fifteen thousand a year. She had expressed this concern to the dry little man from Washington who had recruited her almost twenty years earlier.

He had tried to reassure her. "Don't worry, Mrs. Binkings," he had said. "What you're doing is very, very important." It was during the atomic bomb scares of the 1950's and Mrs. Binkings had giggled nervously and asked, "What if the Russians bomb us? What then,"

And the man had looked very serious and said simply, "Then everything will take care of itself and none of us have to worry about it."

He had double-checked again with her. Her mother had lived to be ninety-five and her father ninety-four. Both sets of grandparents had lived into their nineties.

Amelia Binkings had been sixty when she took the job. She was almost eighty now.

She watched as the second hand finished its sweep around the clock and the time neared

10:55. She reached her hand for the telephone, anticipating the ring.

Fifty-nine seconds. Sixty. Her hand touched the telephone.

One second after 10:55. Two seconds. Three seconds.

The telephone had not rung. She waited another thirty seconds before she realized that her hand was still on the telephone and it was beginning to ache from being held over her head that way. She lowered her hand to the table and sat there watching the clock.

She waited until the time went past 10:59 A.M. She sighed and, with difficulty, rose to her feet. She removed her gold Elgin wristwatch and placed it carefully on the table, then opened the back door and tottered down the steps into her backyard.

It was a bright spring morning and magnolias filled the air with their honeyed scent. The backyard was small and its little pathway was bordered with flowers, which Mrs. Binkings had to admit to herself were not as neatly trimmed as they should be, but it was so hard these days to bend down and work.

In the far corner of the small yard was a round slab of concrete, surrounded by a low metal fence. In the center of the slab was a twelve-foot-high flagpole. The flagpole had been built by the strange dry man from Washington with a crew that had worked all through one night to finish the job. It had never flown a flag.

Mrs. Binkings started down the narrow path toward the flagpole, but stopped when a voice called out, "Hi, Mrs. Binkings. How you all feelin' today?"

She went back to chat across the picket fence with her neighbor, who was a nice young woman even if she had lived in the neighborhood for only ten years.

They talked about arthritis and tomatoes and how no one was raising children properly anymore and finally her neighbor went back inside and Mrs. Binkings walked to the flagpole, pleased that after all these years she had remembered to take off her wristwatch as the man from Washington had told her.

She pushed open the small metal gate in the fence and stepped to the pole. She untied the cord from the metal bracket on the side of the pole. Her fingers hurt from the effort of loosening the dry, tired old knots.

She gave the cleat a 180-degree turn. She felt it click. For a moment, she seemed to feel the concrete whir under her feet. She paused for a moment, but felt nothing more.

Mrs. Binkings retied the flag rope and closed the small metal gate. Then, with a sigh and a lingering twinge of worry about whether what she was doing was all right, she went back inside. She hoped that the apples she had been peeling in the sink had not already turned brown. It made them look so unappetizing.

In the kitchen, she decided to sit at the table and rest for a moment. She felt very tired. Mrs. Binkings put her head down on her forearms to rest. She felt her breath coming harder and harder, until she realized that she was gasping.

11

Something was very wrong. She reached out her hand for the telephone over the table but before she could reach it, there was a piercing pain in the center of her chest. Her left arm froze in position, then dropped back onto the table. The pain felt like a spear had been stuck into her. Almost clinically, Mrs. Binkings could feel the pain of her heart attack radiating outward from her chest to her shoulders and stomach and then into her extremities. And then it became very difficult to breathe and, because she was a very old lady, she stopped trying. And died.

Mrs. Amelia Binkings had been right. When she had turned the flagpole bracket, the concrete *had* whirred under her feet. A powerful, solar-fed generator had kicked into life after twenty years and begun sending powerful radio signals into the air, using the flagpole as an antenna.

In Europe, red lights went on. In a garage in Rome, in the backrooms of a Paris bakery, in the cellar of a plush London home, and in the laundry room of a small country house.

And all over Europe, men saw the red lights go on.

And prepared to kill.

CHAPTER TWO

His name was Remo and his ears hurt. He would have hung up the telephone but that would probably prompt a personal visit and while Ruby Jackson Gonzalez could cause him unbearable pain by shouting at him over the telephone, in person her voice brought him unbelievable agony.

Carefully, so she would not hear, Remo set the receiver of the telephone on the ledge in the booth and walked back out into the luncheonette where an aged Oriental in a powder blue robe stood looking at the covers of magazines on the rack.

"I can still hear her," the Oriental said, in a voice that seemed to have disapproval built in.

"I know, Chiun. So can I," Remo said. He went back and closed the door of the telephone booth, gently so it would not squeak. He rejoined Chiun, who shook his head.

"That woman could broadcast from the ocean floor with no instrument but her mouth," Chiun said.

"I know," said Remo. "Maybe if we stood across the street?"

"That will not do," said Chiun. He reached out

a long-nailed index finger to riffle the pages of a magazine. "Her voice crosses continents."

"Maybe if I wadded up some bread and shoved it into the earpiece of the phone?"

"Her voice would harden it into cement," Chiun said. He moved his hand to another magazine and, with the long fingernail, flipped the pages. "So many books you people have and none of you read. Maybe you should just do whatever it is she wants you to do."

Remo sighed. "I suspect you're right, Chiun," he said.

Hands clapped tightly over his ears, he ran back to the telephone booth. He pressed the door open with his shoulder. Without uncovering his ears, he yelled into the mouthpiece, "Ruby, stop yelling. I'll do it. I'll do it."

He waited for a few seconds, then released his hands from his ears. Only blessed silence came from the receiver and Remo picked it up, sat on the small stool in the booth and closed the door.

"I'm glad you turned that buzzsaw off, Ruby, so that we can talk," he said. Before she could answer, he added quickly, "Just kidding, Ruby. Just kidding."

"I hope so," said Ruby Gonzalez.

"Why is it these days that whenever I call Smith, I get you?" Remo asked.

"Because that man work too hard," Ruby said. "So I make him go out and play golf and get some rest. I handle all the routine stuff, like you."

"And what about me? Don't I deserve any rest?" asked Remo.

"Your whole life be one vacation," Ruby said.

14

"Ruby, will you go to bed with me?" Remo asked.

"I'm not tired."

"I don't mean to sleep," Remo said.

"Why else would I go to bed with you, dodo?"

"Some women find me attractive," Remo said.

"Some women put cheese in their potatoes," Ruby said.

"You know, Ruby, this used to be just one big happy family. Just me and Chiun and Smitty. And then you came along and ruined everything."

"You be the white man and I be the white man's burden," Ruby said.

Remo could picture her smile, even over the telephone. Ruby Gonzalez was not beautiful but her smile was quick and happily blinding, a flash of white in her light chocolate face. She would be sitting in her office outside Smith's, intercepting phone calls, making decisions, lifting his workload to something small enough for four men to handle, instead of the ten-man duties Smith had handled since Remo had known him.

"All right, Ruby," Remo said. "Tell me what dirty rotten job it is this time."

"It be them Nazis. They got that march there tomorrow and you got to stop it. It going to make America look bad in the world, we let Nazis be marching all around."

"I'm not a negotiator," Remo said. "I don't talk people out of doing things."

"You just do it," Ruby said.

"How?"

"You think of something."

15

"You know, Ruby, in six months you're going to be running the country," Remo said.

"I figured five myself but I can live with six," Ruby said. "Call me, you need anything." Her abrasive voice turned instantly to softly rippling chocolate milk with cornstarch thickeners. "Be good, Remo. Give my love to Chiun."

Remo waited until he was sure she had hung up before he snarled at the telephone, "You don't have any love to give, you hateful thing."

When Remo came out of the telephone booth, the luncheonette operator looked at him with open curiosity. This was Westport, Connecticut, and he was used to having strange people wander in, but someone yelling at a telephone booth across the room would be strange anywhere.

Not that Remo looked strange. He was about six feet tall, with dark hair and deepset dark eyes. He was as lean as a rope and he moved smoothly. Not quite like an athlete, but more like a ballet dancer, the owner thought. Come to think of it, he was kind of built like a ballet dancer in that black T-shirt and black chinos, but he had wrists that seemed as thick around as tomato juice cans. Remo had been coming into the store almost every day for three months to buy newspapers and a copy of the *Daily Variety*, the show business newspaper. The store owner didn't think much of his looks but one day his twenty-five-year-old daughter had been working in the store when Remo was there, and when he left, she ran after him to give him change from a ten-dollar bill.

"I paid with a five," Remo had said.

"I'll give you change for twenty."

"No thanks," Remo had said.

"Fifty? A hundred?"

But Remo had just driven away. His daughter had now taken to parking her car near the luncheonette to catch a glimpse of him, so the store owner guessed that even if he wasn't really handsome, he had something about him that women liked.

"You done with the phone?" he called to Remo.

"Yeah. You want to use it?"

The store owner nodded.

"Let the earpiece cool for a few minutes," Remo said. He walked to where the old Oriental continued to flick through magazines with his fingernails.

"I have looked through all these magazines," Chiun said, glancing up at Remo. The Oriental was aged, with white wisps of hair flitting out from his dried yellow skin. He was barely five feet tall and probably had never seen the fat side of one hundred pounds. "There is not one story in any of them that was written by a Korean. It is no wonder that I cannot sell my books and stories."

"You can't sell your books and stories because you don't write your books and stories," Remo said. "You sit there staring at a piece of paper for hours and then you complain that I'm stopping you from writing because I'm breathing too heavy."

"You are," said Chiun.

"When I'm out in a boat in the middle of the sound?" asked Remo.

"I can hear your asthmatic snorting halfway across the country," Chiun said. "Come. It is almost time."

"You going back there again today?"

"I will go there every day for as long as it takes," Chiun said. "I can get nowhere with all your publishers prejudiced against Koreans, but that will not stop me from writing a movie. I have heard about your Hollywood blacklist. Well, if they have a blacklist to make sure that blacks get work, they can start a yellow list and I can get work."

"That's not what they mean by blacklist," Remo said, but Chiun was already out the door heading toward their car, which was parked illegally along the curbside of the busy Boston Post Road.

Remo shrugged, took his morning quota of papers, and tossed a five-dollar bill on the counter. Without waiting for change, he joined Chiun in the car.

"This is a natural for Paul Newman and Robert Redford," Chiun said. "It is just what they need to make them stars."

"I know I'm never going to read it or see it, so I suppose you better tell me about it. Otherwise, I'll never have any peace," Remo said.

"Fine. There is the world's foremost assassin, the head of an ancient house of assassins."

"You," Remo said. "Chiun, reigning Master of the House of Sinanju."

"Shush. Anyway, this poor man finds himself, against his will, working in the United States because he needs gold to feed the poor and the suffering of his small Korean village. But do they let him practice his noble art in the United States? No. They make him become a trainer, to try to teach the secrets of Sinanju to a fat, slothful meat-eater."

"Me," Remo said. "Remo Williams."

"They found this poor meat-eater working as a policeman and they fixed it up so that he went to an electrical chair but it didn't work because nothing in America works except me. So instead of being killed, he was saved so he could go to work as an assassin for a secret organization which is supposed to fight crime in America. This organization is called CURE and is headed by a total imbecile."

"Smitty," Remo said. "Dr. Harold W. Smith."

"And the story tells of the many misadventures of this meat-eater and the many tragedies that befall him as he bumbles and stumbles his way through life and how the Master, unappreciated and unloved, always manages to save him at great risk to his own valued person, until one day the Master's contributions are finally recognized by a grateful nation, because even stupid countries can be grateful, and America showers him with gold and diamonds and he returns home to his native village to live out his few remaining days in peace and dignity, loved by all, because he is so gentle."

"That takes care of you," Remo said. "What happens to me? The meat-eater?"

"Actually, I have not worked out all the minor details of the movie yet," Chiun said.

"And for this you want Paul Newman and Robert Redford?"

"Absolutely," Chiun said. "This is socko for Newman and Redford."

"Who plays who?" asked Remo.

"Newman will play the Master," Chiun said. "We can do something about those funny pale eyes of his to make them look right."

"I see. And Redford plays me."

Chiun turned in his seat and looked at Remo as if his disciple had begun speaking in tongues.

"Redford will play the head of this super-secret organization who you think resembles Smith," Chiun said.

"Then who plays me? Remo asked.

"You know, Remo, when they make a movie, they hire a woman and they call her the casting director, and she is in charge of finding actors to play all the small, unimportant parts."

"A bit part? That's me?"

"Exactly," Chiun said.

"You got Newman and Redford starring as you and Smith and I'm a bit part?"

"That is correct."

"I hope you meet Newman and Redford," Remo said. "I just hope you do."

"I will. That is why I go to this restaurant, because I hear they eat lunch there when they are in town," Chiun said.

"I hope you meet them. I really do."

"Thank you, Remo," Chiun said.

"I really hope you meet them," Remo said.

Chiun looked at him with curiosity. "Your feelings are hurt, aren't they?"

"Why shouldn't they be? You got two stars playing you and Smith. And me, I'm a bit part."

"We'll get somebody good. Somebody who looks like you."

"Yeah? Who?"

"Sidney Greenstreet. I saw him in a movie on television and he was very good."

"He's dead. And besides, he weighed three hundred pounds."

"Peter Ustinov," Chuin said.

"He doesn't talk like me. His accent's wrong."

"If you're going to pick at everything, we're never going to get this movie in the can," Chiun said.

"I don't want anything to do with this movie," Remo sniffed.

He was still sulking when he stopped his car in front of the YMCA in the center of town. It was almost noon and, across the street, the luncheon line for a small restaurant extended to the corner.

"See that mob?" Remo said. "They're all waiting to see Newman and Redford and they've all got movies to sell."

"None as good as mine," Chiun said. "Raymond Burr?"

"Too old. He can't play me," Remo said.

"Well, if you're going to be difficult," Chiun said. He got out of the car and started across the street for the restaurant's front entrance. While the line extended to the corner, Chiun did not have to wait in line. His own table was reserved for him every day in the back of the restaurant. He had resolved this, on the very first day, with

21

the restaurant owner by holding the man's head in a kettle of seafood bisque.

Halfway across the street, Chiun stopped, then walked back to the car. His face was illuminated with the joy of one who is about to perform a great and good deed.

"I have it," he said.

"Yeah?" growled Remo.

"Ernest Borgnine."

"Aaaaah," Remo said and drove away.

Through his open window, he heard Chiun calling. "Any fat white actor. Everybody knows they all look alike."

The head of the American Nazidom Party called himself Oberstürmbannführer Ernest Scheisskopf. He was twenty-two years old and still had pimples. He was so skinny, the swastika armband kept sliding down the sleeve of his wash-and-wear brown shirt. He wore his black trousers bloused into the tops of his shiny high boots, but his legs were like sticks, without discernible thigh or calf muscle, and the impression the lower half of his body gave was of two pencils shoved vertically into two loaves of shiny black bread.

There was sweat on his upper lip as he faced the television cameras for his daily news conference. Remo watched, lying on the couch in the small house he had rented near Westport's Compo Beach, looking at the television.

"We understand that you dropped out of high school in the tenth grade?" a television reporter said.

"As soon as I was old enough to find out that the schools were trying to stuff everybody's head with Jew propaganda," Scheisskopf said.

His voice was as thin and boneless as he was. Two more Nazis in uniforms stood behind him, against a wall, their arms folded, their narrowed hating eyes staring straight ahead.

"And then you tried to join the Ku Klux Klan in Cleveland," another reporter said.

"It seemed like the only organization in America that wasn't ready to give the country to the nigger."

"Why did the Ku Klux Klan reject your membership?" he was asked.

"I don't understand all these questions," Scheisskopf said. "I am here to discuss our march tomorrow. I don't understand why this town is getting so upset about it. This is a very liberal community, at least when the rights of Jews and coloreds and other misfits are concerned. Tomorrow we are marching to celebrate the first urban renewal project in history and the only one that is known to be an unqualified success. I think all those liberals that like projects like urban renewal ought to be on the streets with us."

"What urban renewal project is that?" he was asked.

Lying on the couch, Remo shook his head. Dumb. Dumb.

"In Warsaw, Poland, twenty-five years ago," Scheisskopf said. "Some people call it the Warsaw Ghetto but all it was was an attempt to improve the living conditions of subhumans, just as all modern urban renewal projects try to do."

23

The room shuddered as Chiun came in and slammed the front door behind him.

"Do you want to hear what happened?" he demanded of Remo.

"No."

"They did not show up again."

"Who cares? I'm watching the news."

Chiun turned off the television.

"I am trying to talk to you and you are watching creatures in brown shirts."

"Chiun, dammit, that's my assignment for tonight."

"Forget your assignment," Chiun said. "This is important."

"Can I tell Ruby you told me to forget my assignment?"

Chiun turned the television back on.

"Being an artist among the Philistines is the cross I have to bear," he said.

The American Nazidom Party was holed up in a house on narrow, twisting Greens Farms Road. They had been talking for weeks about a massive march of thousands, but so far only six had arrived. They were holed up in the house.

They were outnumbered forty to one by the people milling around outside. Thirty of them were pickets protesting the planned march. The other thirty were volunteer lawyers from the American Civil Liberties Union, who were busy showing the protestors restraining orders they had gotten from the Federal circuit courts, which said that everybody had to behave and let the Nazis march as an exercise of free speech.

The picketers and lawyers were also outnumbered by the state police and Westport local police, who ringed the house on all four sides to make sure no one got at the Nazis inside.

And all together, they were outnumbered by the press, who milled around in abject confusion, interviewing each other on the deeper philosophical ramifications of this latest display of white American racism. They all agreed it was bad, but typical, because what else could you expect of a country that had once elected Richard Nixon.

At 10 P.M., the television crews left, followed thirty seconds later by the print media. At 10:02, the protestors left, followed at 10:03 by the ACLU lawyers. At 10:04, the police left. Remaining behind were two tired Westport policemen who sat in a prowl car.

At 10:05, the Nazis looked at the window and saw that the coast was clear, so they sent a guard named Freddy outside to stand on the porch with a nightstick and look threatening. The other five stayed inside. Oberstürmbannführer Ernest Scheisskopf swept the chess pieces off the board and onto the floor. They had set up the chess board in case anyone should look through the window, and he could report that the intellectual Nazis spent their time at an intellectual game like chess. But none of them could play chess; they couldn't remember how the knights moved. One of them now got out the checker pieces and they set the board up to play checkers. Two of them knew the moves and were giving lessons to the others.

At 10:06, Remo arrived and leaned his head into the Westport police car. The two cops looked at him in surprise. They had not seen or heard him coming.

"Long day, huh?" Remo said with a grin.

"Better believe it," the cop behind the wheel said.

"Get some rest," Remo said. His two hands darted out. Each touched one of the policemen in the small hollow between the neck and the shoulder collarbone. Both policemen opened their mouths, as if to yell, then their heads dropped forward as they lost consciousness.

Remo shuffled down the flagstone path to the neat frame house.

Freddy, in full uniform on the porch, stiffened to attention as Remo approached.

"Who are you?" he demanded.

"I'm from the *Jewish Standard*. I want an interview," Remo said.

"We give no interviews to the Jewish press," Freddy said. He jabbed at Remo's midsection with the nightstick.

The dark-eyed man did not move, but inexplicably, the nightstick missed his belly.

"Don't do that," Remo said. "That's not nice."

"In the new day to come, we will not be nice to you people either," Freddy said. "Get used to it."

He pulled back the nightstick and this time jammed it full force at Remo's stomach. Still Remo did not move, but somehow the nightstick missed his stomach and slid by alongside his hip.

"I said, stop that," Remo said. "I've been sent here to negotiate. Now behave yourself."

"I'll negotiate," Freddy snarled. He raised the

26

club over his head to smash it down across Remo's skull.

"That's it," Remo said. "That's what I get for trying to be a nice guy."

The nightstick swung down toward his head. Then Freddy felt it being removed from his hand. He felt himself being swung around, then felt the blunted edge of the club at his left ear. He saw the thin man's fist wad up into a club and swing at the other end of the nightstick. The first blow jammed the nightstick into Freddy's ear. His other ear worked well enough to hear two more thuds of Remo's fist. Then he heard nothing more as the club passed through his brain and the large end exited out of the ear on the other side of his head.

"Guggg, gugggg, gugggg," Freddy said as he sank to his knees, the club protruding from both sides of his head, like scooter handles.

"What'd you say?" Remo asked.

"Guggg, gugggg, gugggg," Freddy repeated.

"L'chaim," said Remo.

He knocked on the door and heard feet shuffling about inside.

"Who's there?" asked a voice from behind the locked door.

"Herr Oberlieutenantstürmbannführergauleiterreichsfieldmarshall O'Brien," Remo said.

"Who?"

"Come on, it's too long to repeat. Open the door."

"Where's Freddy?"

"Freddy's the guard?"

"Yeah. Where is he?"

27

Remo looked at Freddy, down on his knees, the long thick nightstick protruding from both ears.

"He's busy right now," Remo said. "But he identified me."

"I want to see your identification," the voice said.

"Freddy's my identification," Remo said.

"I don't want to hear that. Just slide your identification under the door."

"It won't fit," Remo said.

"It'll fit. Just slide it under."

"All right," Remo said.

Inside the room, the five Nazis looked at the door. They heard a scratching sound at the bottom of it. Something began to slip under it into the room. The something was pink. And then there were four other things just like it. They were fingers. Then a hand. Then a brown shirt.

"Oh, my god, that's Freddy," said Ernest Scheisskopf. The men jumped to their feet to run to the door. Freddy's arm, flattened as if it had been run over by a steamroller, was through the crack at the bottom of the door. It kept moving into the room. It was as if Freddy had been photographed and the picture had been mounted on cardboard. Now strings of blond hair came through the crack, and there was a splintering sound as Freddy's skull began to break to fit under the door, but the door shuddered, the wood creaked, and the door flew back off its hinges, into the room, landing on the floor like a thick wooden rug.

Remo stood in the doorway. At his feet was the

rest of Freddy. The five Nazis stared at the night-stick imbedded in his skull.

"Hi," Remo said. "I told you it wouldn't fit."

"*Guggg, guggg, guggg,*" said Scheisskopf.

"That's what Freddy said," Remo explained.

"Who are you?" one Nazi sputtered.

"What do you want?" another called out.

"What did you do with Freddy?" came another voice.

"Just a minute," Remo said. "We're not going to get anywhere with everybody talking at once. Me first. You." Remo nodded to Scheisskopf. "Stop throwing up and listen to me."

"*Guggg, guggg, guggg,*" Scheisskopf said as he continued to spray the room with Arthur Treacher's Fish & Chips.

"Stop it, I said," Remo said.

Scheisskopf swallowed a deep breath and tried to stop retching. He wiped the specks of food off his face with his uniform shirt sleeve.

"Is there any way I can convince you not to march tomorrow?" Remo asked. "I was sent here to negotiate."

"No chance," said Scheisskopf. "Never."

"Don't be hasty," Remo said. "I convinced Freddy."

"Never," Scheisskopf snarled again. "We march for freedom and for the rights of white men everywhere. We march against the race-mixing . . ."

"Goodbye," said Remo.

He grabbed Freddy by the nightstick and dragged him into the room. The two biggest Nazis came at Remo, waving billy clubs. He hit them with Freddy and they went down in a lump.

The next two came at Remo with lead-filled blackjacks. He moved between the two of them, spinning between them, moving forward and back, closer and farther away and, when they both knew he was in range, they swung at him with wild roundhouses. Remo moved low, beneath the plane of their swings and, like a shot and its immediate echo above him, he heard the twin splats as each of them slammed the blackjack into the other's skull, with the old reassuring sound of temple bones being crushed and splintered.

Remo nodded and moved out from between them, as they fell forward, locked on each other for a moment, then slid loose as their two bodies thumped onto the floor.

Oberstürmbannführer Ernest Scheisskopf was backing into a corner. In front of him, he held for protection a *Muhammad Ali vs. Superman* comic book. A large black "X" had been drawn through Ali's face on the cover.

"You get away, you," he squeaked. "I'll call the police. I'll tell."

"Look, Ernest," Remo said. "Don't get upset. Don't just look at it like you're dying."

"How should I look at it?" Scheisskopf said.

"As one giant leap for mankind," Remo said.

When he was done, Remo tidied up, then left, pulling the broken door back into the door opening behind him. It was three miles to his house at Compo Beach and he decided to run back. He hadn't had any exercise in a long time.

Chiun was as Remo had left him an hour earlier, sitting in the center of the floor, a large piece of parchment on the floor in front of him, a quill pen poised over an ink bottle as if ready to strike. There was not a word on the paper.

"What was it tonight, Chiun?" Remo asked, pointing toward the blank parchment. "People playing their radio too loud in Venezuela?"

"I worried so much about you, it was not possible to work," Chiun said.

"Worried about me? You called them creatures in brown shirts before. You didn't sound impressed."

"Don't bicker," Chiun said. "It is taken care of?"

"Of course."

"Good," Chiun said. "These Nazis are vile things."

"Not these tonight. Not anymore. And since when are you down on Nazis? If the House of Sinanju could work for Ivan the Terrible and the Pharaoh Ramses and Henry the Eighth, why not Nazis? Or wouldn't they pay your price?"

"The House of Sinanju refused to work for them. Just the opposite. We volunteered our services to get rid of their leader. The one with the funny mustache."

"A freebie? Sinanju?"

Chiun nodded. "There are some kinds of evil that cannot be tolerated. It is not a frequent thing we do to volunteer our services, because if I do not get paid, the village does not eat. But this one time we did and the lunatic heard that the House of Sinanju was coming so he took poison.

Untidy to the last, he managed to kill his female companion first." Chiun spat his disgust.

"I will never get any work done," he said, "since you seem determined to chatter at me. I'm going to sleep."

"Sweet dreams," Remo said.

It was a glorious day for a parade. The sun rose, bright and busy, burning off the morning residue of Connecticut's long winter chill.

The Boston Post Road in Westport was lined with thousands of people carrying baseball bats, empty bottles, tomatoes, and tire chains. The American Civil Liberties Union had called for volunteers from all over the country and there were four hundred lawyers running up and down the projected line of march reading from court orders that there must be no violence. No one paid any attention to them.

There were three hundred police in full riot gear. Parked along the parade route were four ambulances and two morgue wagons.

Hawking their way up and down the parade route were peddlers selling American flags. Some of the more adventurous had stocked a small supply of Nazi armbands for sale, but so far they had received no requests for them.

The planned Nazi parade had everything.

Except Nazis.

Remo noticed this when he drove to the luncheonette to pick up Chiun's copy of the *Daily Variety*. At the house, he gave Chiun the *Variety* and turned on the television. It was an hour past the scheduled time to start the parade and some of the press had finally gone over to the Nazis' house on Greens Farms Road.

The television air was filled with bulletins. The Nazi cadre had been murdered during the night. The bodies of the six brownshirts, including one who was partially flattened, had been found imbedded in an inside wall of the house. They looked like fish trophies, one reporter said. Their bodies had been arranged in two interlocking triangles, the traditional Star of David.

"This is terrible," Chiun said.

"I thought it was kind of neat," Remo said. He smiled as he heard that the Zionist Defense League had claimed credit for the killings.

"A disaster," Chiun said.

"I thought it had touches," Remo said. "I liked the idea of the Star of David."

"Silence. I am not talking about your stupid games. Did you see what *Variety* said today?"

"What did they say?"

"They said that Robert Redford is out in Colorado making speeches about Sun Day."

"Good for him. Everything needs a little encouragement once in a while."

"And Paul Newman is practicing to race an automobile in Florida."

"Ummmmmm," said Remo, watching the television pictures of the Nazi house on Greens Farms Road.

"Why are they not here?" Chiun demanded.

"I don't know, Chiun," Remo said.

"Why have I been here for months eating seafood soup that I hate, waiting to see them?" Chiun asked.

"Don't know," Remo said.

"I have been deceived."

"It's a deceitful world."

"Only this part of it," Chiun said. "Only the white part of it. This would never happen in Sinanju."

"Nothing happens in Sinanju," Remo said.

"If I ever see Newman and Redford, I will peel them like grapes," Chiun said.

"Serve them right."

"Even worse," Chiun said. "I will not let them star in my epic."

"That'll teach them."

"I'll get someone else," Chiun said.

"Good," said Remo.

"I'll get Brando and Pacino," Chiun said.

"Good for you. Don't take this lying down."

"I won't. Oh, the perfidy of it all," Chiun said.

"That's show biz," Remo said.

CHAPTER THREE

Dr. Rocco Giovanni walked into the attached garage of his small house in Rome and opened the trunk of his Fiat. He noticed the car's dark blue paint starting to purple, and he hoped he could get another year out of it before it turned so bizarre a color he would have to get the auto repainted.

Inside the trunk was a leather doctor's bag. It was old and beaten. The black leather, despite careful and frequent oiling by Dr. Giovanni, had begun to crack and there were thin tan lines on the bag where the leather's innards had begun to show. The bag had been a gift to him when he graduated medical school almost twenty years earlier and he had carried it with pride ever since.

It was the bag he carried on those three days a week when he worked in the clinic for the poor he had built in one of Rome's worst slums. He slammed the trunk lid shut.

Inside the car, he started the motor, listened to it cough hesitantly, then with obvious reluctance come to life.

He breathed the small sigh of relief he always breathed when the car started.

He pressed the button that activated the garage door and as he put the car in reverse, he glanced up casually at the wall in front of the car. Then he put the gear shift back in neutral.

A red light was blinking on the wall. Doctor Giovanni's first thought, after twenty years, was: So that's what it looks like when it comes on. He had never see it lit before.

He watched. The red light flashed once, long, then two shorter flashes, then three even shorter flashes. There was a pause, then it repeated the one-two-three sequence.

He watched the light for a full minute until he was sure in his own mind that it was flashing in a clear, unmistakable pattern. He realized his hands were clenched tight on the steering wheel and he forced himself to relax his grip.

Finally he sighed and turned off the car's motor.

He removed the key, got out, and put his old leather bag back into the trunk.

Then he walked over to a shiny new Ferrari, which sat in the other half of the garage. From its trunk, he took another doctor's bag, this one rich brown cordovan, highly polished and glistening in the dim overhead light of the garage. It was a bag he replaced every six months, even though in such a brief period of time, it had not even begun to show signs of wear. It was just that his wealthy patients expected that everything about him should be new and rich. Only the poor trusted a doctor with holes in the soles of his shoes, and only because they had to.

Dr. Giovanni started the car's engine, which roared powerfully to instant life. He let the car idle as he went back into the house.

His wife, Rosanna, looked up surprised as he came back into the kitchen.

"What'd you forget now, Rocco?" she asked. She smiled at him from the kitchen sink where she was rinsing dishes before putting them in the automatic dishwasher.

"This," he said. He came close behind her and kissed her lightly on the neck. His arms went around her trim body and squeezed her lovingly.

"You already kissed me goodbye," she protested mildly. "You horny thing."

"Do you know how much I love you?" he asked.

"Sometimes I get the hint," she said. She turned and he took her in his arms and kissed her hard on the mouth.

"I love you forever," he said.

"And I love you, too," she said. "And if your patients weren't waiting, I'd show you how much."

He looked in her eyes and she thought she saw a glint there of something she had never seen before, then he buried his lips against her throat, said a muffled "goodbye" and left.

When she heard the car pull out of the garage, she walked to the front window. She was surprised to see the Ferrari pulling away. He hated that car and had only bought it to impress his wealthy patients, whose riches helped finance the real love in his life, the free clinic he ran for the poor.

His nurse and receptionist were surprised to see Doctor Giovanni show up at his private offices only a few blocks from the Vatican, but he sloughed off their unspoken demands for an explanation about his presence.

Inside his office, he called a young doctor who owed him a favor and arranged for the other doctor to handle the patients at Giovanni's free clinic.

Next he dialed the number of the Russian embassy. When he mentioned his name, the call was transferred directly into the Russian ambassador's office.

"Doctor Giovanni, how are you?" the ambassador said in guttural Italian. He managed to make the musical language sound like German.

"I'm fine," Giovanni said. "But I have to talk to you."

"Oh? What's wrong?"

"Your blood tests just came back," the doctor said, "and we must discuss them."

"Is something wrong?"

"Not on the telephone, Ambassador. Please."

"I will be right there."

While he waited, Doctor Giovanni took something from his office safe and put it into the bottom of the leather medical bag. Then he folded his hands on his desk and rested his head on them.

The ambassador was there in less than ten minutes, accompanied by his ever-present bodyguard, a hawk-faced man who viewed everyone and everything with suspicion. Parking meters, restaurant checks, street peddlers, he watched them all as if each were capable of overturning the glorious Communist revolution. He followed the ambassador into Doctor Giovanni's office.

"Can he wait outside, please?" the doctor said.

The ambassador nodded. With obvious reluctance, the bodyguard went into the waiting room where he leaned against the wall next to the door to the doctor's private consulting room.

The receptionist glared at him. He stared back blankly, until he forced her to turn her eyes away.

"I know what it is," the ambassador said. "The saintly doctor has decided to defect to Mother Russia." He was smiling but there was a faint film of nervous perspiration on his forehead.

Giovanni smiled back. "Not just yet," he said.

"Ah, but someday," the ambassador said. "You and your free clinic. Your modest life. You are the most communistic of all."

"And that is why I could not live in Mother Russia," Doctor Giovanni said. "Please sit here."

He pulled out a chair and sat the ambassador on it, facing an X-ray display board. Onto the glass screen, he put two large chest X-rays.

He flicked on the switch for the display panel and turned off the office light.

"These are your most recent X-rays," he said. "They were taken when you had that slight chest cough during the winter." As he spoke, Doctor Giovanni walked behind the ambassador toward his desk.

"You'll notice the slight darkish spots at the bottom of each lung," he said. He opened the brown leather bag and reached into the bottom.

"Yes. I see them. What does that mean?" the ambassador asked nervously.

Doctor Giovanni's hand closed on the butt of a pistol.

He walked up behind the ambassador.

"Nothing," he said. "Absolutely nothing." Then he put a bullet into the Russian's skull from behind the left ear.

Doctor Rocco Giovanni was glad the gun had worked after all these years.

The report of the pistol resounded through the small consultation room. Outside, the nurse and receptionist looked up at the unusual loud sound.

The Russian bodyguard reached under his jacket for his gun and pushed through the unlocked door into the inner office.

But before he could do anything, Doctor Rocco Giovanni raised the pistol to his own right temple and squeezed the trigger.

The gun worked again.

CHAPTER FOUR

When Admiral Wingate Stantington came through the private entrance to his office, his secretary intercepted him.

"Here it is," she said, holding out her hand. There was a shiny brass key on it.

"All right," he said. "And you've got the other one?"

"Yes, sir."

"You put it in a safe place?"

"Yes, sir."

"Better tell me where it is, in case I lose this one and something happens to you."

"It is in my top left desk drawer, in the back, behind my box of Tootsie Rolls."

"It'll be safe there?"

"Yes, sir. Nobody goes in my desk."

"Okay. Thank you." He took the key and dropped it into his jacket pocket.

"And there's somebody waiting to see you, Admiral."

"Oh? Who is it?"

"He wouldn't give his name."

"What's he look like?"

"Like Roy Rogers," the secretary said.

"What?"

"He does, Admiral. He's got on a ten-gallon hat and tooled boots with the pants tucked in and he's got a gabardine shirt with white piping all over the chest. If he was a woman, he'd look like Dolly Parton."

"Send him in right away," Stantington said. "No, have him wait a minute. I want to test this bathroom key first."

Stantington was sitting behind his desk when his visitor came in, looking like everybody in the Country Music Hall of Fame.

"Well, well. Vassily Karbenko," Stantington said, as he rose, leaned across the desk, and extended his hand. The Russian was as tall as Stantington and his handshake was bony and firm. He kept on his carefully blocked cowboy hat.

"Admiral," he said. Even his voice had a slight western coloration.

"And how are things on the cultural attache front?" Stantington asked.

The admiral smiled at his visitor as they stood, facing each other across the broad desk.

"I haven't come to discuss culture, Admiral. Perhaps the lack of it instead." Karbenko had a small smile around his lips, but his eyes were cold and narrow, and his voice was frosty.

"What do you mean, Colonel?" Stantington asked.

"Have you been briefed this morning?" Karbenko asked.

Stantington shook his head. "No. I just got here. You want to use my bathroom? I've got a key."

"No, I don't want to use your goddamn bathroom. I want to know why one of your spies assassinated our man in Rome today." He glared across the desk at Stantington, a look so intense it seemed to exert a physical pressure on the CIA director, who slowly sank back into his leather chair.

"What? I don't understand."

"Then I'll make it very clear. The Russian ambassador to Rome was assassinated this morning by an Italian doctor who was one of your men."

"Our men?" Stantington shook his head. "It couldn't be. It can't be. I would know about it."

"His name was Rocco Giovanni. Does that ring a bell?"

"No. Is he in custody?"

"No. He killed himself before we could get to him," Karbenko said.

"Rocco Giovanni, you say?"

Karbenko nodded.

"Wait here a minute," Stantington said. He put his new brass key on the desk. "Use the bathroom if you want." He passed through his secretary's office and into the office of his chief of operations.

"What the hell is going on here?" he asked.

The operations chief looked up, startled.

"What, Admiral?"

"This Russian ambassador killed in Rome. Is that ours?"

The operations chief shook his head. "No. Not ours. Some doctor, looks like he went crazy, shot the ambassador and himself. But he wasn't one of ours."

"His name was Rocco Giovanni," Stantington

43

said. "Check that name out right away and call me inside. The goddamn top Russian spy in the United States is in my office and I'm catching hell."

When Stantington returned to his office, Karbenko was sprawled in a chair in front of his desk, his legs extended before him, his hat pulled down over his face.

"I'll have something in a moment," Stantington said.

The two men sat in silence until the buzzer flashed. Stantington picked up the telephone and listened.

After a few moments, he replaced the telephone and looked up with a smile. "Your information is wrong, Comrade. Rocco Giovanni was not one of ours. There is no record in our personnel listings of a Rocco Giovanni."

"Well, you can take your personnel listings and shove them," Karbenko said, sitting erect in the chair and dropping his tan hat on the thickly carpeted floor. "CIA money sent Giovanni to medical school. CIA money helped him open a clinic in Rome. For twenty years, he's been subsidized by CIA money."

"Impossible," said Stantington.

"But true," said Karbenko. "We've got the proof. We even know what code he was working under."

"What was that?" asked Stantington.

"Project Omega," Karbenko said.

"Never heard of it," said Stantington. Then he paused. Project Omega. He *had* heard of it. When? Where? It came back to him. Yesterday.

He had heard of it and ordered it disbanded because no one knew what it was.

"Project Omega, you say?"

"That's right," said Karbenko.

"And you know about it?"

"All we know is its name. It's in our files from Khrushchev days. We know it was fronted by some foundation that spreads CIA money around."

"You're not going to believe this," Stantington said.

"Probably not."

"But you know more about Project Omega than we do."

"You're right, Admiral. I'm not going to believe that."

"I'm serious. I cancelled Project Omega yesterday because nobody knew what it was."

"Then you better find out quickly what it is," Karbenko said. "I think it goes without saying that my government responds a little more actively to this kind of provocation than yours does."

"Now don't get upset, Vassily," Stantington said.

"Don't get upset? One of our most important diplomats is murdered by one of your agents and you tell me not to get upset. This is, I take it, the new morality you have all brought to Washington."

"Please."

"My government will likely respond in kind," Karbenko said.

"Show some faith in us."

"Oh, yes. Faith. As in the Bible you are all so fond of quoting these days. Well, some of us can quote your Bible too."

"I hope you're going to say 'love thy neighbor.' "

"I was about to say 'an eye for an eye, a tooth for a tooth.' "

Stantington stood up. "Vassily," he said, "there's only one way I can convince you I'm telling the truth. I want you to come with me."

Karbenko grabbed his cowboy hat and followed Stantington out of the room. They took an elevator to the basement of the building, transferred to another elevator which took them to a sub-basement and then into another elevator which took them even further into the ground.

"America is a marvelous country," Karbenko said.

"How so?" asked Stantington.

"You people can never leave well enough alone. For years it was sufficient for an elevator to go up and down, from the bottom to the top. Not any longer. I have been in hotels in this country and if you want to ride from one floor to the next floor, you have to ride elevators up and down for fifty floors. Do you know, in the World Trade Center in New York you have to ride four elevators to get from the top to the lobby? I suppose this is taught in your engineering schools. Creative and Imaginative Elevator Design."

Stantington saw nothing funny about this. He led Karbenko out into a hallway.

"You are the first Russian ever to be here," the CIA director said.

"That you know of," the Russian agent said drily.

"Yes. That's quite true."

Stantington led Russia's top agent in the United States down a long maze of corridors, lined regularly and with steel reinforced doors. There were no names on the doors, only numbers.

Behind door 136, they found a balding man sitting behind a desk, his head buried in his hands. He looked up as Admiral Stantington came in. His face wrinkled in disgust and he put his head back into his hands.

"I'm Admiral Stantington," the director said.

"I know," said the man, without looking up.

"You're Norton, the head librarian?"

"Yes."

"I'm looking for a file."

"Good luck," Norton said. He waved toward another door on the far side of the office.

Stantington looked at the man whose eyes were still cast down toward the desk top, then he looked at Karbenko and shrugged.

They walked to the far door. Stantington pulled it open. It led into a room almost a city-block square and twelve feet high. All the walls were lined, floor to ceiling, with file cabinets and there was an island of cabinets in the center of the room.

But this room looked as if a gang of particularly mischievous elves had been at work in it for a hundred years. All the file drawers were open. Papers were strewn about, in some places piled into five-foot-high mounds. Manila folders were tossed everywhere. Papers had been crumpled, others ripped and torn.

Stantington stepped into the room. He kicked aside papers that stacked up around his feet and ankles like autumn leaves after a windstorm.

"Norton," he bellowed.

The thin bald man came up behind him.

"Yes, sir?" he said.

"What's going on here?"

"Maybe you'll tell me," Norton said bitterly.

"That will be just about enough of your surliness," Stantington said. "What happened in here?"

"Don't you recognize it, Admiral? It's part of your new open door policy. Remember? You were going to show how open and aboveboard the new CIA was operating so you announced you were going to honor the new freedom of information law. The public was invited. They came at me like locusts. They all had your statement in their hands. They tore everything apart."

"Didn't you try to stop them?"

"I tried to," Norton said. "I called the legal department but they said we'd need a court order to stop them."

"Why didn't you get it?"

"I asked the lawyers to. They drew straws to see who would go to court."

"Why?" Stantington asked.

"Because they said whoever handled the case would probably have his balls cut off. By you. Probably be indicted."

"All right, all right. So who lost?" Stantington asked.

"Nobody," Norton said. "They all used the same size straws."

"What are you going to do?" asked Stantington. "How long have you been here anyway?"

"Since the CIA started right after World War II," Norton said. "And what I'm going to do is wait till garbage day and then throw all this out in Hefty bags. And then I'm going to sweep the floor one last time and then I'm going to take my retirement and then, hopefully, I'm going to have the nerve to tell you to shove the CIA, your open door policy, and the freedom of information law up your ass. Will that be all?"

"Not quite. I'm looking for a specific file," said Stantington.

"Tell me what it is and I'll have the garbage men keep an eye out for it."

Norton was moaning as he walked back to his desk.

"Freedom of Information," Karbenko said softly. "I can't believe you did this. Do you know how we handle our secret information in Russia?"

"I can guess."

"I doubt if you can even guess," the Russian spy said. "We keep it all in one building. It is surrounded by a high, thick stone wall. The stone wall is surrounded itself by a high electrified fence. If, somehow, you get to the fence and touch it without being electrocuted, you get shot. If you get over the fence, vicious dogs will tear you apart, if you don't get shot. You get shot if you touch the wall. You get shot if you climb the wall. You get shot if you come near the building. If you get inside the building, you get tortured and shot. We shoot the members of your family for good measure. Also any friends we can think of. And here . . . you hold open house." He whistled his amazement. "Tell me, Admiral, are you really running the CIA or is this the "Gong Show'?"

"I truly appreciate you telling me how to do my job . . ." Stantington said.

"Somebody better," Karbenko interrupted. "You keep firing agents and weakening this agency and before you know it, somebody in the world is going to get adventuresome because they'll think the United States is a toothless tiger."

"Somebody like Russia?"

"Perhaps," said Karbenko. "And that would be a tragedy for all of us," he said thoughtfully.

"Come on," said Stantington, leading Karbenko out. On his way, he growled at Norton, "Don't you touch a piece of paper inside there. I'm sending some men down here to work on something."

Back upstairs, Stantington told his chief of operations to get everybody in the building down to the record room to find anything they could about Project Omega.

"Only those people with top secret security clearances, you mean?" the operations chief said.

Stantington shook his head. "I said everybody and I meant everybody. Just because some poor employee of ours isn't cleared for top secret, why should he be the only one in the country who doesn't know what's in our secret files? Hurry it up. We'll be waiting."

Stantington and Karbenko sat silently in the

admiral's office for thirty minutes. There was a knock on the door and Stantington buzzed in the chief of operations. The man's eyebrows raised when he saw Vassily Karbenko sitting across from the director's desk.

"I can come back," he said.

"Don't worry about it," Stantington said. "Vassily knows all our secrets. What'd you find out about Project Omega?"

"In that whole room, there's only one piece of paper that mentions any Project Omega. It's a personnel file."

"And what does it say?"

"All it says is that Project Omega was an action plan, designed for use in the event America lost an atomic war. That's all it is.

"Whose personnel file is it in?" the admiral asked.

The chief of operations looked at Stantington and rolled his eyes toward Karbenko. "Should I say that, sir?"

"Go ahead," Stantington said.

"It was a former employee who's retired now. He apparently had something to do with the plan."

"And who is this former employee?"

"His name was Smith. Dr. Harold W. Smith. He lives now in Rye, New York, and runs a mental health sanitarium named Folcroft."

"Thank you," said Stantington. When the chief had left the room, the admiral looked at Karbenko and held his hands open in front of him.

"Vassily, see? We don't know any more about it than you do."

"But Project Omega killed our ambassador nevertheless," Karbenko said. "That could be considered an act of war. You are, or course, going to contact that Doctor Smith?"

"Of course."

The telephone buzzed on Stantington's desk. He picked it up, then handed it to the Russian.

"For you."

"Karbenko here." The Russian listened and Stantington saw his ruddy tan complexion seem to pale. "I see. Thank you."

He handed the telephone back to the CIA director.

"That was my office," he said quietly. "Our ambassador in Paris was just stabbed to death. By a baker. He is one of yours. Project Omega again."

Stantington dropped the telephone onto the floor.

CHAPTER FIVE

After Vassily Karbenko left his office, Admiral Stantington had his secretary track down the telephone number of Folcroft Sanitarium in Rye, New York. She buzzed him on the intercom to tell him she had gotten through to Doctor Smith's office.

Stantington picked up the telephone.

"Hello," he said.

A woman's voice answered "Hello."

"Is Doctor Smith there?"

"Not to just anybody what calls," the woman said. "Who is this?"

"My name is Admiral Wingate Stantington. I am the . . ."

"What do *you* want?"

"What I don't want is to waste time talking to a secretary. Please put Doctor Smith on the line."

"He's not here."

"Where is he?" Stantington asked. "This is important."

"I made him go out and play golf. That's important, too."

"Hardly," said Stantington. "I want him to return my call immediately and then come to see me," the CIA director said.

"He gonna be busy. You come and see him," Ruby said.

"Really. Miss, I am the director of the Central Intelligence Agency."

"That's all right. He'll see you anyway. That's figuring you can get here without getting lost. When I was with the CIA, I didn't notice anybody who could get anywheres without getting lost."

"You? Worked for the CIA?"

"Yes," said Ruby Gonzalez. "And I was the best you had. When should I tell the doctor that you be coming?"

"I'm not coming. He's coming here."

"You're coming," said Ruby as she hung up. She waited for a moment, then picked up the telephone and dialed Westport, Connecticut, whistling softly under her breath.

It would be a simple matter, Stantington knew. He could just send a few agents over to Folcroft or to the golf course or wherever this Doctor Smith was hanging out and pick him up and bring him to Washington. And if he didn't want to come willingly, well, that could be arranged too.

Except . . .

Except that it was extra-legal, outside the law, and not quite in keeping with the new CIA that Stantington was dedicated to creating.

He decided that he needed guidance on the subject and it had better come directly from the top.

If he was going to be breaking any laws, the orders to do it should come from the President. Stantington was new to Washington, but he had spent a lifetime in the Navy and had learned all the secrets of grabbing glory, when glory was being distributed, and making sure someone else's ass was in the sling when it was ass-in-the-sling time. Now some deep-remembered instinct was telling him that the one way to make sure the President didn't saw off a limb with you on it was to make sure that the President was out on the same limb. Even if he had been your old school chum and your old service buddy.

It never occurred to Admiral Wingate Stantington that there might have been a time in Washington when things were done differently and better. When people charged with the safety and security of the nation did what they knew had to be done and didn't spend all their time looking over their shoulders, watching for someone who was getting ready to hand them up.

As he drove into Washington the words of the former CIA director rang in his ears: "One day they'll change the rules in the middle of the game and your ass'll be grass, just like mine. I'll save you a spot in the prison chow line."

That's what he had said. It had sounded like a threat and already it seemed to be turning into a prophecy. Only on the job a few days, and Stantington was already facing decisions that he knew could make or break him. He felt something a little more like sympathy for his predecessor.

The President was waiting for him in the Oval Office and Stantington felt a tinge of relief when

55

he saw the familiar slope-shouldered figure wearing an open-collared shirt and a light blue cardigan sweater. The role reversal was strange. He had been ahead of the President when they both went to the Naval Academy and later he had been the younger man's commanding officer on assignment to sea duty. The younger man had always looked up to Stantington as a leader and as a commander.

But now, here he was, the President, the Commander-in-Chief, and Stantington felt relief at being able to dump his problem in the Presidential lap. It was the almost-mystical power the office had. Stantington had no children but he thought this must be the way children feel when they turn a problem over to their parents. That sense of there, *now* it'll be taken care of.

"How you doin', Cap?" the President asked in his soft voice. "Sit down."

"All right," Stantington said. He lounged easily in the chair in front of the big mahogany desk.

"So who's killing all these Russians?" the President asked.

"You heard about it?"

"State told me. That's why I figured you were on your way here." The President paused for a moment and Stantington nodded.

"Well, Mister President, I don't quite know how to tell you this," said Stantington.

"Try me." The President lounged back in his chair, holding a yellow wooden pencil between the fingertips of both hands.

"You asked who's killing all these Russians. I think maybe we are."

The President came half up out of his chair. The pencil dropped from his fingertips, unnoticed, to the floor.

"We what?"

Stantington raised his hands as if warding off an invisible enemy. Then he quickly sketched out for the President what had happened to the two ambassadors and Vassily Karbenko's visit to his office that morning.

"Why in the name of anything that's holy did you end Project Omega?" the President asked.

"Just following orders, Mister President," said Stantington.

"I don't remember giving any orders like that."

"But you did say you wanted to cut out the waste in the CIA. You said that at your press conference when I was confirmed, remember? And what's more wasteful than a project like this one where nobody knows anything about it or what it's supposed to do?"

"The only thing more wasteful might be World War III," the President said. "And if Russian ambassadors keep getting killed off by our people, that's just what we're going to have."

A heavy silence descended on the room.

"What about the woman in Atlanta?" the President asked.

"That's the first thing I did, sir. My men found her in her house. She died. It looked like a heart attack. There was nothing in the house that could tell us anything."

"You sent your men in to search the house?"

Stantington realized that he had already broken a law by doing just that. When he went on trial, he knew, he could talk about fears of World War III, but a jury five years from now wouldn't want to know about that. All they'd want to know was that he had illegally sent CIA agents breaking into the house of an American citizen without a warrant and without proper authorization.

"Yes, sir," he said. "I did that."

"I didn't authorize that," the President said.

An alarm bell went off in Stantington's head. He knew what the President was doing. He was dissociating himself from the CIA director's actions.

The hell with that, Stantington thought. He didn't get to be an admiral because he hadn't known how to play the game.

"Are you telling me, sir, that I did wrong?"

"Yes," the President said. "What you did was technically wrong."

"I think, then, that I ought to make amends," said Stantington, thinking fast. "I think I will announce to the press what I did and apologize to the American people. If I do it now, I might minimize the damage." He looked at the President to see if the threat had registered. Such a statement by Stantington might well topple an administration whose popularity, according to the polls, was the lowest in thirty-five years of post-war administrations.

The President sighed.

"What do you want from me, Cap?" he said.

"I want you to have authorized that entry into that old woman's house in Atlanta."

"Okay. I authorized it. Satisfied?"

"For now," said Stantington. "But it'd be nice to get it in writing. No hurry, of course. Anytime today would be fine."

"You don't trust me," the President said.

"It's not that. We've been friends a long time. It's just that I met the old CIA director yesterday. In jail."

"Where he belongs," the President said.

"For doing just what I did today," said Stantington. "I don't want to join him. In writing today will do nicely."

"All right," said the President. "You'll have it. Now what else about Project Omega? You can't mean that you haven't one word about it in all your files?"

Stantington decided not to tell the President about the havoc that the new director had wreaked on the CIA's secret files with his freedom-of-information policy. No sense in bothering the commander-in-chief with too many details.

"Only one reference," he said.

"And that is?"

"The program was started back about twenty years ago by a CIA employee, now retired."

"Who's the employee?" the President asked.

"His name is Smith. Harold Smith. He's some kind of a doctor and he runs a sanitarium named Folcroft. In Rye, New York."

The President's face tensed, then opened into a slow wide smile.

"Doctor Smith, you say?"

"That's right."

"Did you talk to him?" the President asked.

"I tried to but I got his secretary and she told me he was out. A nasty thing, she was. She said she used to work for the CIA."

The President nodded.

"She sounded like she was black," Stantington said.

The President just smiled.

"What did she tell you?" he asked.

"Snotty little snippet. She told me that Smith wouldn't come to see me, but I should come to see him. I told her that that was impossible, but she said that I would come to see this Smith, whoever he is."

"Like a threat?" the President said.

"More like a promise," Stantington said. "She was a cool thing. Do you mind, Sir, if I ask why you're smiling?"

"You wouldn't understand," the President said.

"Is there something special you want me to do?"

"Not really," the President said. "Just keep trying to find out whatever you can. I'll speak to the Soviet ambassador and assure him of our total confusion about this whole matter. And you exhibit all possible speed, Cap."

"Aye, aye, sir," said Stantington, rising to his feet. "Anything else?"

"No. Oh. Did you wear a topcoat to work today?"

"I carried one. I thought it might rain. Why?"

"You might need it. It gets cold in Rye, New York."

"Are you telling me to go there, Mister President?"

"No," the President said. "It's out of my hands."

When he left the Oval Office, the director of the CIA was even more confused than he had been before. And he had a peculiar feeling that the President knew something about this Doctor Smith that he wasn't telling.

Alone again in his office, the President of the United States considered whether or not he should go upstairs to his living quarters and take the dialless red telephone out of the dresser where it was hidden, pick it up, and speak to Smith.

For Admiral Wingate Stantington had been right. The President did know something about Smith that the CIA director didn't. The President knew that Smith had not just simply retired from the CIA, but had been tapped by another young President to head up a secret agency called CURE, whose job it would be to work outside the Constitution to try to preserve America's Constitution. The young President had felt that America needed a helping hand in fighting crime and corruption and internal unrest.

This new President had been briefed on the agency by his predecessor. He hadn't liked it. The thought of a secret agency running around, out of control, frightened him. And what made it even worse was that the President could not give assignments to CURE. He could only suggest.

Smith, the only head of the agency since its inception, made the decisions about what CURE would work on.

The new President had thought of disbanding the agency immediately. That was the one order he was allowed to give it. But before he could do that, he found himself needing CURE and its Doctor Smith and the enforcement arm, Remo, and the aged Oriental who seemed able to do magic. And that was when the President first heard of Ruby Gonzalez, too, the CIA agent who had helped CURE bail America out of a sticky situation and then had been fired by the spy agency for her trouble.

The President had never met Ruby but he felt as if he knew her and if she had told Wingate Stantington that he was going to go to Rye, New York, he had no doubt that Wingate Stantington's next stop was Rye, New York.

The President drummed his fingers on the desk for a few moments, then decided not to call Smith. Not just yet. Not until Stantington had spoken with him. Instead, he picked up the telephone and told his secretary to summon the Russian ambassador. Perhaps he could express his regrets and apologies for the deaths of the two ambassadors and, using all the selling power at his command, convince the Russian that it was a mistake and that America was trying to stop it.

As he replaced the telephone, he thought of Doctor Smith forced out onto the golf course by Ruby Gonzalez. Good, he thought. He hoped Smith enjoyed his round.

It might be the last game of golf any of them would ever play.

As he rode along, suspended in air, Wingate Stantington thought that it was all very strange.

He had gotten back to the CIA's Langley headquarters and as he was leaving the chauffeured limousine some instinct told him to take his top coat.

Alone in his office, he threw the coat across the back of a chair and for the first time that day, with a little peace and quiet, was able to use his private bathroom, using his private key to his private door with the private lock that cost $23.65 and to hell with *Time* magazine.

His pedometer showed only three miles. He had walked only three miles and, by this time of the day, he should be up to seven miles at least. One's duty always had a way of interfering with one's goals, he thought.

Inwardly, he still seethed at the thought of the President, his life-long friend, trying to finesse him and get him to shoulder all the responsibility for the break-in into that old lady's house in Atlanta. As they had so often that day, his thoughts turned again to his predecessor, languishing in jail for not doing much more wrong than Stantington had already done that day before lunchtime.

He telephoned the CIA's top staff lawyer.

"Hello," the lawyer said.

"This is Admiral Stantington."

"Just a moment, sir." There was a pause. The admiral knew the lawyer was turning on a tape recorder to transcribe the call. It angered him. Didn't anybody trust anybody in Washington anymore?

"Yes, sir," the lawyer said. "Just had to put down my coffee cup."

"Didn't realize it took two hands," Stantington said. "When the question of parole arises for the former director . . ."

"Yes, sir."

"My position is that he should be paroled as soon as possible. No further worthwhile purpose is served by keeping him in prison. Do you understand?"

"I do, Admiral."

"Thank you." Stantington hung up and for the first time that day felt good.

Then he heard a sound inside his bathroom. It was water running in the sink.

Had he left the water on?

He walked to the bathroom door, opened it, then stopped in the doorway, unsure of what to do.

There were two men inside his bathroom. One was young with dark hair and eyes. He wore a black T-shirt and black chino slacks. The other was an aged Oriental wearing a blue brocade kimono. He was pressing the large round gold cap that turned off the water in the sink, and then lifting it to turn it on. He did it again.

"What . . . who . . .?"

"Shhhh," the Oriental told Stantington without looking at him. "This is a very good faucet, Remo," he told the man behind him.

"Chiun, somehow I knew you'd like it. It's gold."

"Do not be crass," Chiun said. "There is only one knob to play with. Most faucets have two knobs. This only has one. What I do not understand is how you can control hot water and cold water with only one knob."

"Who are you two?" Stanington demanded.

"Do you know how this faucet works?" Chiun asked the CIA director.

"Err, no," Stantington said. He shook his head.

"Then you be quiet. Remo, do you know?"

"Something to do with a two-way valve, I suppose," said Remo.

"That is like saying that it works because it works," Chiun said.

"I'm calling the security guards," Stantington said.

"Do they know how this works?" Chiun asked.

"No. But they know how to throw you the hell out of here."

Chiun turned away as if Stantington was not worth talking to. Remo said to the CIA director, "If they don't know anything about faucets, don't call them."

Chiun said, "Telling me that it has something to do with a two-way valve is no answer at all, Remo." He lifted the faucet and the water came on; he pressed down on the handle and it turned off.

Finally he sighed, the wisdom of the ages having surrendered in the face of modern toilet technology.

"Congratulations," he said to Stantington. "You have a wonderful bathroom."

"Now that the inspection's over, would you mind telling me what this is all about?" Stantington said.

"Who knows?" Remo said. "Work, work, work. From the minute I get up in the morning till I go to bed at night. Always something. They must think upstairs that I've got four hands. So, let's go."

Admiral Stantington made it very clear that he was going nowhere, not with these two. He was still making it clear when he found himself being hoisted into a green Hefty garbage bag.

"Chiun, fix it so he can't yell, will you?" Remo said and Stantington felt a light pressure of a single fingertip on the underside of his jaw. Not yell, hah? He'd show them yelling. The admiral opened his mouth to shout for help. He breathed deep and let the air come rushing out. There was no sound, except for a thin hiss. He tried again, breathing harder this time, but still producing only silence.

He felt himself being hoisted up in the air. He heard Remo say, "Is that his topcoat, Chiun?"

"It is not mine," Chiun said.

"Get it, will you? It might be chilly in Rye," Remo said.

It was all very strange. That was what the President had said to him when he asked about the topcoat. There was something going on in government that Stantington didn't know about.

The topcoat was dumped unceremoniously on

top of his head. He heard the garbage bag being fastened with a yellow plastic zipper closure.

The bag was hoisted in the air. He must be on Remo's shoulder, he decided, because he could hear the man whistling and the sound was very close to his ear. He was whistling the theme from *The Volga Boatman.*

He heard the door to his office open and they walked outside.

Remo's voice said, "Hi, honey. The admiral in?"

"Yes, but he's busy," a woman's voice answered. It was Stantington's secretary. The CIA director wanted to call out that he was not in his office; he was in the garbage bag. He tried, but still no sound came out.

"Well, that's all right," he heard Remo tell the secretary. "We'll come back later."

"You can wait if you want," the young woman said. Even through plastic, Stantington could recognize unmistakable lust in her voice. "I'll make you coffee," she told Remo.

"No thanks, he said.

"I can get you Danish. Two Danish and coffee. Or I could make you sandwiches. It wouldn't be any trouble at all to make you sandwiches. All I've got to do is drive to the store in town and get some cold cuts and some bread. I could be back here in no time and I'd have good sandwiches for you. Liverwurst. With Vandalia onions and mayonnaise."

"Aaaaagh," Chiun said in disgust.

"Honey, when I come back for you, it won't be with sandwiches in mind," Remo said.

Stantington heard his secretary exhale a puff of air. She must have leaned back in her chair because it squeaked slightly under her weight.

Ask him what's in the bag, he wanted to shout. But he was mute.

"Give us a pass out of here, will you?" Remo said. "You know what pains in the butt all these guards and things are."

No, no, Stantington tried to shout. Nobody gets in or out, without all kinds of clearances. Somebody doesn't just come up to your desk and ask for a pass out. Follow the book, girl. But no sound came from his mouth and he heard his secretary say, "Sure. Here. Take this. It's the admiral's special clearance pass. Just flash that in anybody's face and nobody'll bother you."

"Thanks, toots," Remo said.

"And if you want to come back and see me, well, just hang onto that pass. It'll get you right in."

It must be mind control, Stantington thought. This Remo, whoever he was, must have some kind of power to hypnotize. Otherwise his secretary would never be so lax with security procedures.

"You can count on it," Remo said. "This will be my prized possession." Stantington shifted slightly. Apparently Remo was taking the pass from the woman. He felt himself leaning forward inside the bag, then heard Remo drop a kiss on his secretary's cheek.

Then he was lifted high up again and felt himself moving. A strange thought passed through his mind. He would have expected riding in a bag on someone's shoulder to be bumpy as the person's body dipped with each step he took. But he felt like he was floating. There was no jarring, no real sense of movement.

He heard his secretary's voice behind him. "Hey, what's in the bag?" she asked.

"Government secrets," Remo said.

"Come on, kidder. Really. What's in the bag?"

"The admiral," Remo said.

The secretary giggled and then her voice faded as the door to the outside office closed behind them.

"You're doing good, Admiral," Remo said. "Just behave and you'll be out of there before you know it."

No one challenged them in the halls or the elevators and then they were outside, because Stantington heard the plastic of the bag rip slightly and he breathed the sweet fresh air of the Virginia countryside. He gulped deeply, then wondered to himself if this Remo didn't ever get tired. Stantington was a big man, over 200 pounds, and Remo just kept walking along carrying him on his shoulder with no more effort than if he had been an epaulette on a military uniform.

Then there was an automobile and then an airplane, and then a helicopter. Through the three rides, the white man and the Oriental kept bickering. Something about starring in a movie. The Oriental quoted *Variety* to prove that the white man could not expect more than three points of the gross and 1 percent of 100 percent of the wholesale price on commercial products. He talked a lot about bringing it all home for under five mill and Remo would get his money *pari passu* and that was the best he could do. Remo said he could have lived with Burt Reynolds or Clint Eastwood, but Ernest Borgnine was an insult.

Stantington was beginning to believe he was in the hands of lunatics.

Then he was dumped onto a hard floor and the top of the bag was ripped open.

He heard a voice that dripped acid ask, "What is this? What are you two doing here?"

"Don't go blaming me," came Remo's voice. "Ruby told me to do it. It was all Ruby's idea."

"That is right, Emperor," Chiun said. Emperor? What Emperor, Stantington wondered. "I heard her tell him," Chiun said. "I was away across the room and I could still hear her over the telephone, telling him to do it. Her voice was so loud, it ruined my writing for the day."

"That's right," a woman's voice said. "I told him to do it."

"Do what?" asked the acid voice. Stantington stood up. His legs were wobbly and weak from the hours of being cramped into the bag.

The acid voice came from a thin balding man sitting behind a large desk, in an office surrounded by windows tinted smoky brown. Stantington recognized them as one-way glass. From the inside, they were windows. From the outside, they were mirrors. Stantington looked through them and saw the waters of the Long Island Sound, down a long embankment from the upper-story office he was in.

The balding man's eyes widened when he saw the CIA director.

"Stantington," he said.

Stantington opened his mouth to speak.

"Ga, ga, ga, ga, ga," he said.

"Chiun," said Remo.

The tiny Oriental, not even coming up to Stantington's shoulder, stepped forward and gently pressed a spot under the admiral's jawbone. There was no sense of pain, no feeling of anything internal having been tampered with. But one moment he could not talk and the next moment he knew his voice had returned.

"Doctor Smith, I presume," Stantington said.

He looked around the office. Remo and Chiun were standing behind him, along with a tall, light-skinned black woman. Her hair was wrapped in a red bandana. She was wearing a black pants suit and her face was more actively intelligent than beautiful.

Smith nodded. He looked to Ruby. "Suppose you tell me what this is all about," he said.

"He wanted to talk to you. I told him you was too busy," Ruby said, "so I sent these two to go get him."

"In a Hefty bag?" Smith said.

"Why not?" said Ruby. "Nobody notice just one more bag of garbage coming out of that CIA. That CIA be all garbage." She looked challengingly at the admiral.

Remo said to her, "Why are you wearing that hanky on your head?"

"Because I like it," Ruby said. "I like to wear a hanky on my head. You think I fix my hair up for you? No. I fix my hair up for me. Today I felt like wearing it like this. You don't like it?"

71

Stantington noticed her voice had started at shrill and escalated rapidly to ear-piercing, without ever having paused at human. Remo covered his ears with his hand.

"Stop," he said. "I surrender. Stop."

Ruby took a deep breath. She was ready to deliver the second fusillade when Smith called her name sharply.

"Ruby."

She stopped.

Smith glanced at Stantington. "I imagine you would feel better speaking to me alone."

Stantington nodded.

"Would you all mind waiting outside?" Smith said.

When the office had cleared, Dr. Smith motioned Admiral Stantington to a seat on the sofa. There were no chairs in the office but the one behind Smith's desk.

Stantington said, "Suppose you begin by telling me what this is all about."

Smith looked at him coolly, then shook his head. "You seem to have forgotten, Admiral. You wanted to talk to me."

"And you had me brought here in a plastic bag," Stantington said. "That merits me an explanation."

"Chalk it up to employee overexuberance," Smith said, "and it merits you absolutely nothing. Please state your business."

"I've been kidnaped, you know," Stantington persisted. "That isn't exactly a laughing matter."

"No," Smith agreed slowly. "But *you* would be if you ever mentioned it. Being taken out of your office in a Hefty bag. Your business, please?"

Stantington stared hard at Smith who sat, ceramic-still. Finally, the CIA director sighed.

"I ran across your name in our files," he said.

"That's right. I was once with the company," Smith said.

"This was in connection with something called Project Omega."

Smith moved forward onto the edge of his seat.

"What about Project Omega?" he asked.

"That's what I want to know. What in the hell is it?"

"It really doesn't concern you," Smith said.

"It costs me almost five million a year out of my budget and it doesn't concern me? Agents sitting around three hundred sixty-five days a year playing cards and it doesn't concern me? One telephone call a day to a little old lady in Atlanta, Georgia, and it doesn't concern me?"

"Have you been tampering with Project Omega?" Smith asked. His eyes were narrowed and his voice was frozen.

"I've done more than tamper," Stantington said hotly. "I put those slackers out of business."

"You did what?"

"I cancelled the project. Fired the agents. Closed it down."

"You imbecile," Smith said. "You arrogant, cement-headed imbecile."

"Just a minute, Doctor," Stantington began.

"We may not have a minute, thanks to your

bumbling," Smith said. "Did the President authorize closing down Project Omega?"

"Not exactly."

"Weren't you aware that there is a notation in the CIA's permanent records that Project Omega can be closed down only on the specific written authoriziation of the President of the United States?"

Stantington thought about the CIA file room, the shambles of papers and records strewn about the floor.

"But that's right," Smith said in disgust. "You couldn't find anything in your files, could you? Not after you decided to make the CIA into some kind of exercise in participatory democracy and your record system was destroyed."

"How did you know about that?" Stantington asked.

"That's immaterial," Smith said, "and not germane to this conversation which involves your other most recent lunacy in dealing with Project Omega."

"Since it's been closed down," Stantington said, "two Russian diplomats have been killed. The Russians are blaming it on us. They say that both assassins were on our payroll."

"That's right," said Smith. "They were." He spun around in his chair and looked out the one-way windows toward the Sound. "And that's not the worst of it. The Russian premier is on the hit list, too."

"Oh, my god," Stantington said. He slumped back in the couch. "How can we stop it?"

Smith turned back. His face still showed no emotion.

"We can't," he said. "Once Project Omega has been set in motion, it can't be stopped."

CHAPTER SIX

A faint buzz seemed to come from under Smith's desk. As Stantington watched, the thin man reached under his desk to press a button. A desk drawer opened and Smith reached into it and lifted out a telephone receiver.

"Yes, sir," he said.

He listened for a moment, then said, "Yes, sir. He's here right now."

He listened again and then shook his head. "It is very serious trouble. Very serious."

He paused.

"If you wish, sir," he said. "Project Omega was started in the late 1950's when Mister Eisenhower was President. It was after our U-2 spy plane had been shot down. Russia was getting edgy and there was a serious possibility that it might launch a first-strike nuclear attack against the United States. You must remember, sir, that this was a time when Russia had no world enemy but us."

As he spoke, Smith looked at Stantington with displeasure.

"The President and Khrushchev met privately on a yacht off the Florida coast. Yes, sir, I was at the meeting. That was necessary because President Eisenhower had assigned me to implement Project Omega.

"At that time, the Russians had been developing some new types of voice analyzers to determine when a person was lying and President Eisenhower had asked Mister Khrushchev to bring one aboard. He asked the Russians to turn it on and then he told the premier that America understood the possibility of a first-strike attack by Russia on our country.

"The President reminisced. He said that when he was a victorious general, he still feared for his life. He lived in dread of a random bullet just passing his way that might kill him. No matter how powerful a man became, he said, dying was never easy. 'Some day,' he told Mister Khrushchev, 'you might decide to launch an attack on America. You might even defeat us. That is possible,' he said. 'But what is not possible is that you will live to enjoy it.' Mister Eisenhower said that he was not talking about some doomsday device to destroy the world. 'We do not want to kill the human race,' he said. 'But Russia's top leaders will die. You may win a first-strike war,' he told Khrushchev, 'but it will mean personal suicide to you or your successor and your top people.' Mister Eisenhower hoped that this kind of threat might help to avoid atomic war just a little longer, and that time might bring peace."

Smith listened and nodded again. "Yes, sir. Khrushchev accused Eisenhower of bluffing but the lie analyzer showed that the President was telling the truth."

Stantington listened in disbelief as Smith continued talking.

"The sole purpose of Project Omega in the CIA was to launch the killers in the event of our losing an atomic war. No, sir, the program wasn't meant to be perpetual. It was designed to last exactly twenty years. By my calendar, sir, it would have ended next month and no one would ever have known. But Admiral Stantington's budget cuts have now done what atomic war didn't do. It has turned loose killers on the Russian leadership."

Stantington felt his stomach drop into his groin. Suddenly, the air-conditioned air in the office smelled bitter to his nostrils.

"There are four targets, sir. The ambassadors to Paris and Rome. They have already been disposed of, as you know. The Russian ambassador in London and the Russian premier himself remain."

Smith shook his head.

"No one knows, sir. The assassins were recruited by another CIA man, long since dead. Yes. His name was Conrad MacCleary. He died almost ten years ago. He was the recruiter and the only one who knew who the assassins were."

Smith listened for long minutes as the CIA chief fidgeted on the cheap, Scotchgard-treated sofa.

"No," Smith finally said. "It is a matter of the utmost gravity. I would recommend that we immediately notify the USSR of the danger to the two remaining men." He paused. "Yes, sir. We can handle that. I don't think anyone else has the capability." He looked at Stantington. "Most especially the CIA."

The admiral flushed.

Smith said, "Yes, sir." He extended the telephone toward Stantington. "It's for you," he said.

Stantington rose and walked across the office. He could feel his pedometer clicking against his hip as he strode. He took the telephone.

"Hello."

The familiar Southern voice bit into his ears like an electric drill.

"You know who this is," the voice said.

"Yes, Mister President," Stantington said.

"You will do nothing about Project Omega, do you understand? Nothing. I will handle what has to be done diplomatically. What has to be done in the field will be done by others. The CIA will remain out of this. Totally and one hundred percent out of it. You have it, Cap?"

"Yes, sir."

"Now I suggest you get back to Washington. Oh, another thing. You will forget, totally forget, the existence of Doctor Smith, Folcroft Sanitarium, and Rye, New York. Got it?"

"Yes, sir," Stantington said. The telephone clicked off in his ear.

Stantington handed the phone to Smith who put it back in the desk drawer, which closed with a heavy-locking click.

Smith pressed the buzzer on his desk. Stantington did not hear anyone enter but Smith spoke.

"You will escort the admiral back to the helicopter so he may return to Washington."

Stantington heard Remo's voice. "He doesn't have to go in the Hefty bag?"

Smith shook his head.

"Good. I don't like schlepping things around all the time. Not even for you, Smitty."

Chiun's voice said, "Some people are suited only for the most meager forms of work."

"Knock it off, Little Father," Remo said.

"Get him out of here," came Ruby Gonzalez's voice. "These CIA people gives me a headache."

CHAPTER SEVEN

But Admiral Wingate Stantington had already told someone of Doctor Harold Smith's existence.

Vassily Karbenko sat on a bench on a foot-bridge over the Potomac River. The spires and domes and statuary of official Washington were behind him. His long legs were sprawled out in front of him and his ten-gallon hat was pulled down over his face. His thumbs were hooked into the tunnel belt loops of his blue cord trousers and he looked as if he would be altogether at home if he were sitting on a straight-backed wooden chair, leaning against the wall on a wooden porch in front of the Tombstone sheriff's office a hundred years earlier.

From his early youth, Vassily Karbenko had been tagged for big things. He was the son of a physician and a genetic scientist and in his teens after World War II, he had been sent to study languages in England and France. While in England, he had seen his first American movies and had become an instant fan of the old American West. It seemed to be the life all men should have—being a cowboy, working the range, sleeping next to a campfire at night.

"If you like America so much, defect," his roommate told him one night.

"If it weren't for my parents, I might," said Karbenko. "But who said I liked America? I just like cowboys."

He returned to Russia when his studies were completed, just in time to see his parents marched off to a workcamp in one of the Stalinist purges. Russian science at the time was securely in the hands of a fraud named Lysenko, whose approach to genetics and heredity was that there was no such thing as genetics and heredity. Believing that an organism could alter and perfect itself in its own lifetime might have made for good Communist politics, but it was awful science. It was twenty years before Russia's agriculture program began to recover from the hole Lysenkoism had dug for it.

Still, while he was a zero as a scientist, Lysenko was a very astute politician and when Vassily Karbenko's father challenged his scientific know-nothingism, it was the senior Karbenko and his wife who were marched off to Siberia.

Ordinarily, this kind of blot on the family record should have ruined whatever chance young Vassily had to move up in the Soviet system. But Stalin himself was soon gone, shot by some of his most trusted advisers, and almost as a reaction to that, Vassily Karbenko found himself riding a wave of promotions through the Soviet spy system, aided by his friendship for a minor party bureaucrat who had inexplicably risen to become the Soviet premier. Along the way, Vassily found out that his parents, like millions of others, had been executed in Russian slave camps.

Karbenko had not yet adopted his cowboy style of dressing. That came when he was assigned to the United States in the early 1970's.

It could have been one of the tragedies of his life to find, when he got to America, that there were very few real cowboys left and none of them were like those in the movies he had grown up with.

But by this time, he had come to a new realization. In the 1970's, spies were the cowboys of the world. Working for a government, yes, but basically on their own, responsible in the end for what they did and not how they did it.

Karbenko was a very good spy and a very dedicated Russian. But he still wore his cowboy suits, like a display of mourning clothes, for a world he had been born too late to enter.

Karbenko heard footsteps coming along the footbridge toward him and he tilted up the corner of his hat to notice the Russian ambassador to the United States heavily puffing his fat way toward him.

Anatoly Duvicevski sat next to Karbenko, took a handkerchief from the breast pocket of his well-cut single-breasted suit, and mopped the sweat from his brow.

"You aren't exactly difficult to spot in that costume, Karbenko," said Duvicevski. He made no effort to hide the disapproval in his voice.

"The fellow down to the right, reading the newspaper. He's one of them. There's another in the telephone booth at the end of the bridge to the

85

left," Karbenko said. "The one you passed without noticing."

Duvicevski glanced left and right.

"So the Americans know we're meeting," he said.

"But of course they know we're meeting, Comrade," Karbenko said. He drawled the "comrade" so it sounded like "pardner." "If the Americans can't hold a secret meeting in Washington, why should we be able to? It comes down to the fact that this is a nice day and this is a pretty spot for a meeting. The air is fresh and the birds are singing. Should we meet in a stuffy office somewhere and inhale each other's cigar smoke? And for what purpose? Because they will still know that we met."

Duvicevski grunted. Karbenko reassured him by clapping a large bony hand on his knee.

"So what happened?" he asked the still-sweating ambassador whose face had broken out in a second round of sweat.

"I just left the President. He explained Project Omega to me."

"Explain it to me," said Karbenko.

"It is a Doomsday plan that the Americans thought of in the fifties. It was supposed to go into action if they lost an atomic war but it has gone into action now and they do not know how to stop it."

"We have two diplomats dead," Karbenko said. "How many more targets are there?"

"Just two," said Duvicevski. He looked at the Russian spy with narrowed eyes. "The ambassador to England and the premier."

Karbenko whistled. "You have already so advised the Kremlin?"

"Of course," said Duvicevski. "The premier is under special security guard. And all types of extra personnel have been assigned to protect the ambassador in London."

"How has the Kremlin received this news?" Karbenko asked.

"All our forces around the world are being put on standby, for a full combat alert. I understand there is now the highest level strategy meetings going on to determine whether or not to publicly blame the United States for these two dead ambassadors."

"What do you think?"

"I think if anything happens to our premier, some hothead in the Kremlin will push the button that will begin World War III. If that happens, you and I will be dead here in Washington, Karbenko."

"Did the President say anything else?"

"He offered us the use of some 'special personnel' he called them, to protect the premier and the ambassador. Of course, I turned him down. I assured him we could protect our people ourselves."

Karbenko thought for a moment.

"What kind of special personnel?" he asked.

"He did not say."

The two men sat silently, staring out over the bridge railing at the greasy waters of the Potomac. It was typical of what was wrong, and right, with America, Karbenko thought. A beautiful natural gem of a river that had been turned into a garbage dump and an oil slick because no one had thought to protect it. And now, it was finally being reclaimed by a massive expenditure of time and effort and money. No other civilized country in the world would have let the river get so bad. And no other country in the world, faced with so bad and dying a river, could have been able to mount the effort and the resources to reclaim it. America was a land of violent pendulum swings and much of the national energy was spent correcting excessive movements in one direction or another.

"Do you believe him?" Karbenko finally asked.

"Do you take me for a fool? Of course not. Who would believe so childish a story?"

"I do," said Karbenko.

The sweating little egg of a man turned toward the tall raw-boned Soviet spy.

"You aren't serious, Vassily."

"Look at it for a moment. If they just wanted to knock off some of our ambassadors, would they have used people we could trace to the CIA? People who've been drawing CIA money for twenty years? There are mercenaries all over the world that anybody could hire for such jobs. And no one would be the wiser. No. The story is too preposterous not to be true."

Duvicevski popped a cough drop into his mouth.

"You believe the President?" he asked.

"Yes," said Karbenko. He smiled. "Didn't he once say he'd never lie to us?"

"He didn't mean us," said Duvicevski.

"I know. But I believe him anyway. And I believe Admiral Stantington when he says he knows nothing about this Project Omega. He knows nothing about anything. God must really love the Americans."

"There is no god," said Duvicevski.

"Our system makes one believe that. The Americans' survival makes one doubt it. By what else but godly intervention could you explain a country that never learns anything but survives anyway?"

"What do you mean?"

"When those terrorists kidnaped and killed that politician in Europe last year, do you know why the police and secret police couldn't find them?"

"No."

"Because the government had been under so much pressure from the left about civil liberties that it had destroyed all its intelligence files. So when the terrorists struck, no one was able to find them. And in New York City a few years ago, there was a tavern bombed by terrorists. A half-dozen people killed. You know why the bombers were never found?"

"Why?" asked Duvicevski.

"Because the New York City police had destroyed all their intelligence files on terrorists because keeping them violated people's civil rights. So killers went loose."

"What has that got to do with anything?"

"Maybe nothing," said Karbenko. "Maybe everything. America never learns. There are so many examples of what bad intelligence or no intelligence can do and still this country panders to the so-called civil rights of people who would destroy the country itself. Stantington is destroying the CIA and the idiot thinks that he is serving America by doing it. That's why I say God must be on America's side. No other country could act so stupidly and survive."

"They are doing our work for us," Duvicevski said.

"No, they're not," said Karbenko. "Time will do our work for us. Given enough time, our system will prevail. All these lunatics like Stantington are doing is creating an unstable world. I know we will conquer a stable world. But an unstable world . . . it may one day be ruled by the kangaroos."

Duvicevski pondered this a while before he said, "So you believe the President and Stantington."

"Yes," said Karbenko. "They are telling the truth as they know it. But the whole story is still a fabric of lies."

"What?"

"There is a man alive now who devised this Project Omega. He did it twenty years ago. Now you tell me how this man devised this program twenty years ago and just now, when it goes into effect, the targets just happen to be our current premier and our current ambassadors to London and Rome and Paris? How did he know twenty years ago who would be our premier? Or our ambassadors? This man knows more than he tells and I do not believe him when he says that he does not know who the assassins are."

"Do you know who this man is?" asked Duvicevski.

"Yes."

"And what do you plan to do?" the ambassador asked.

"I plan to question him myself."

"And?"

"And find out just what it is the varmint really knows," Karbenko said with a large smile.

CHAPTER EIGHT

"I'll tell you, Smitty, you're running some operation here," Remo said. "World War III is getting underway all because of you and where are you? Out on a golf course and you leave Ruby around to run things."

The faintest flicker of an unaccustomed smile brightened Smith's face for a millisecond.

"Ruby is a prize," he said. "I don't know how I did this job all these years without a good number two."

"She's a number two all right," Remo said. "She's a shit. She spends all her time yelling at me."

"Not so loud, Remo," Smith said. "She'll hear you."

Remo glanced toward the closed door of the office, dreading the possibility that it might just burst open and Ruby would march in, assailing his eardrums with her earthmover voice.

"Yes, Remo, not so loud," said Chiun. "She might hear you."

Remo whispered. "I liked it better when it was just you," he said to Smith.

"I didn't think I would ever hear you say that," Smith said.

"Emperor," Chiun said, "Remo has nothing but the highest regard for you. He often tells me this, that he would work for no one but you at these wages."

Smith recognized the start of a pitch for more money and interrupted quickly.

"You're both going to England," he said. "I want you to get in close and protect that Russian ambassador."

"I should think you'd be worrying about the Russian premier instead," Remo said.

"I am, but I can't get permission to send you to Russia," Smith said.

"And you have permission to send us to England?" Remo said.

"Not exactly. But I can get you to England."

"You can get us to Atlantic City, too," Remo said. "Why not send us there? They've got casino gambling now."

"Or Spain," Chiun said. "Spain is nice in the spring. And a Master of Sinanju has not been in Spain since the time of El Cid. I think the Spanish could probably use us well. The Spanish were always good."

"England," Smith said.

Remo looked at Chiun. "Whenever we're supposed to go someplace, you always want to go to Persia for melons," he said. "Why all of a sudden Spain?"

"Because Persia is now Iran and the melons are no longer any good and we tried working for the Persians and they are idiots," Chiun said. "I thought you and I might look around in Spain. El Cid was really very good. Until Sinanju went to work for him, he could do nothing right, but then we straightened things out for him and he chased out the Arabs. We made him a star."

"I don't believe it," Remo said. "Charlton Heston would never have anything to do with the House of Sinanju."

Chiun ignored that. "We gave him Valencia," he said.

"Sure," said Remo.

"We made him what he is today," Chiun said.

"He's dead," Remo said.

"Exactly," said Chiun. "A terrible tragedy."

Remo turned back to Smith. "That means El Cid tried to stiff the House of Sinanju on their fee, and they turned on him. You better make sure that Thanksgiving shipment of gold to Sinanju is never late."

"It's always on time," Smith said. "And now you're going to England.'

"I don't want to."

Smith pressed the buzzer on his desk. "Ruby, would you come in here, please?"

Remo stuck his fingers in his ears.

Ruby entered the office.

"Remo doesn't want to go to England," Smith told Ruby. "Would you please convince him to go?"

Ruby started. Remo pressed his fingers harder into his ears. It was no use. He could not drown her out. If he pressed his fingers in any farther and any harder, he would puncture his own eardrums.

He waved his hands in surrender.

"There be a plane at Westerchester County Airport waiting for you," Ruby said. "You better be getting there fast."

"It's not Westerchester. It's Westchester," Remo said sullenly.

"Whatever it is, the plane's waiting there for you. Get a hop on, 'cause if you miss it, you be in big trouble."

"I'll fix you for this, Smitty," Remo said. "Some night, I'm going to pour quick-setting cement down her throat so she can't yell at me anymore and then I'm coming back for you."

"Fine," Smith said, "but first go to England. And make sure nothing happens to that Russian."

Remo and Chiun left Folcroft Sanitarium in the backseat of an institutional car. They did not see the man in a ten-gallon hat sitting behind the wheel of a red Chevrolet Nova parked near the Folcroft entrance. Ruby, watching Remo and Chiun leave from a front window, did and wondered what somebody in cowboy clothes was doing parked near Folcroft. She called the front gate and told the guard to be very casual about it but to write down the license number of the parked car.

Just in case.

They were the only two passengers on the private twin-engined jet that nosed around immediately toward the east and began humming its way across the Atlantic.

Chiun sat by the window, staring at the wing. He had once told Remo he was amazed at how well the western world had done in stumbling on a good design for an aircraft, but he also believed that nothing done by a white man was ever fully correct. So if the design was good, the wings must be loose. On flights, he always sat by the window, staring at the wings as if willing them to stay on.

Remo folded his arms and sat back in his soft leather seat, determined not to enjoy the flight.

"How the hell are we going to defend some Russian when we don't know if we'll be able to get to him and we don't know who we have to defend him from?" he grumbled.

"It was in the days just after Wang, the first great Master of Sinanju," Chiun said.

"What was?"

"The Great Wang had had much success in bringing the services of Sinanju to many places and accumulating gold to help care for the weak and the poor of the village. But then he died, as all men must. And in the prime of his life, too. Barely eight decades of life had he lived.

"Sinanju was young then, too, and those who had asked the help of our House thought that the secrets of Sinanju had died with the Great Wang. They did not know that each Master trains his successor. Some are fortunate to have good students, respectful and obedient. Others are less fortunate."

"You're getting ready to pick at me again, Chiun, and I won't stand for it. I didn't pick you; you picked me. And you only did it because there wasn't anybody in Sinanju good enough to teach," Remo said.

Chiun ignored him.

"So after the death of the Great Wang, there was no more work, and without work there was no gold. Soon the village was hungry again. We were preparing to send the babies home to the sea."

Remo grunted. Hard times in Sinanju, for scores of centuries, had always been accompanied by "sending the babies home to the sea"—tossing newborns into the North Korea Bay to drown because there was no food for them to eat.

"The new Master was Ung. He was a quiet man, much given to the writing of his poetry."

"He's responsible for that dreck you're always reciting at me?" Remo said.

"You are gross, Remo. You are really gross. It is well known that Ung poetry marks one of the high points in the history of literature."

"Three hours of unky-punky grunts about a flower getting ready to open? Bull-whipple," Remo said.

"Silence. Listen and perhaps you may yet learn something. The Master Ung, with sorrow, put aside his pens and realized he must do something to save the village.

"Now it happened at this time that there was a Japanese warlord who was usurping the property of many other lords around him. And this warlord did greatly fear for his life because there were many who wished his death. This story did reach our village and the Master Ung heard of it, and left for that faraway country. Before he left, he sold his writing implements and his many poems so that the village could be fed."

"Selling those poems wouldn't keep the village in Saltines for ten minutes," Remo said.

"Over the seas he traveled, and Ung went to the Japanese warlord and offered to protect him from his enemies. The warlord had heard of the Great Wang and since this was his successor, he contracted with Ung to protect him. For an attempt to kill the warlord in his sleep had been made just the night before, and the Japanese knew he was in mortal peril.

"Still he did not know which of his enemies were trying to kill him. There was a family to the north and a family to the south and a family to the east and a family. . ."

"To the west?" said Remo.

"Yes," said Chiun. "You have heard this story before?"

"No."

"Then be silent. There was a family to the north and a family to the south and a family to the east and a family to the west, and the Japanese warlord did not know which of them might be trying to kill him, because all had reason to fear his reckless and ruthless ambitions.

"But Ung spoke to the warlord in his poetic way. 'When bulls break down fences,' he said, 'sometimes rabbit steal corn.' The warlord thought of this for many hours and then he understood what Ung meant, and he began to think which of his own court might try to kill him so that he himself could take the warlord's place.

"The more he thought of it, the more he came to suspect his eldest son who was evil and cruel, and that night he turned Ung's hand against the son and the son was no more. But still later that night, another attempt was made to kill the warlord in his sleep and only the swift intervention of Master Ung saved the Japanese's life.

"The warlord then felt bad that he had suspected his eldest son unjustly but he came to think some more and he realized that it was his second oldest son who was even more evil and cruel than the first-born son. And he turned Ung's hand against that second son.

"But still there was another attempt on his life, again foiled only by Ung's arrival at the very last moment.

"And so it went. One by one, Ung removed the seven sons of the warlord, seven evil young men who, if they had been elevated to the position of warlord, would have been even more ferocious than their father and even more brutal than he in their dealings with their neighbors.

"And when the seventh and last son was dispatched, the warlord and Ung met in the great hall of the palace. And the warlord said, 'We have disposed of all my sons, every one. So the danger is removed and I am again safe.'

"It was more a question than a statement, Remo, since the Japanese are a sneaky people and their questions are really statements and their statements are really questions. But Ung answered, 'Not yet. You still face one danger.'

" 'And what is that?' asked the warlord.

" 'The Master of Sinanju,' said Ung who then proceeded skillfully and quickly to kill the warlord. Because, Remo, you see, this was his contract from the four lords whose lands surrounded those of the troublesome one. They wanted him dead, along with his bloodthirsty sons so they could be assured that they would live in peace. And this was how Ung chose to do it. The Great Ung himself had been responsible for the nightly attacks upon the warlord."

Then Chiun was silent, still staring out the window at the plane's left wing.

"So?" asked Remo.

"So? What so?" said Chiun.

"You can't stop a story like that," Remo said. "What does it mean?"

"Is it not obvious?" asked Chiun, finally turning his hazel eyes toward Remo.

"The only thing obvious is that the Masters of Sinanju are always mean, duplicitous men who can't be trusted," Remo said.

"Trust you to misunderstand," Chiun said. "Sometimes I don't know why I bother. The moral of the story is that it is hard to defend yourself against an assassin when you do not know who the assassin is."

"Chiun, that doesn't tell me a damn thing I didn't already know. We know how hard it's going to be to protect the ambassador when we don't know who the button man is."

"You see nothing else in that story?" Chiun asked.

"Not a damn thing," Remo said.

"There is another moral," Chiun said.

"Namely?"

"Danger comes wearing no banners. And the closer it is, the more silent it will be."

Remo thought for a moment. "Who will watch the watchman?" he suggested.

"Exactly," said Chiun, turning back to the window.

"Little Father?" said Remo.

"Yes, my son," Chiun said.

"That story stinks."

"One cannot describe a stone wall to a stone wall," Chiun said mildly.

It was damp and cold when Remo and Chiun stepped into a cab in the heart of London. Water dripped from Lord Nelson, his statue black in the night, high over the black stone lions of Trafalgar Square.

"How much to the Russian embassy?" Remo asked the cabbie, a warted man with a sweat-soaked cotton cap.

The embassy was only nine blocks away on Dean Street, but the cabbie recognized the American accent.

"Four pounds, lad," he said.

"Take me to Scotland Yard," Remo said. "The taxi fraud office."

"All right, mate. Two pounds and not a penny less. And you'll not get a better price anywhere this foul night."

"Okay," Remo said. "Get it moving."

To make it look good, the cab driver took them through Leicester Square and past Covent Gardens before doubling back to Dean Street.

"Here ye be, lad," the drive said when he pulled up in front of a three-story brick building on the quiet cobblestoned street. A cluster of metal piping hung down a wall of the building and a television antenna reached out awkwardly into the black nighttime sky.

"Wait a minute, Chiun," Remo said. "You, too," he told the cabbie.

Remo hopped out of the cab and walked up the three brick steps to the building's front door. The bell was the old-fashioned kind that required manual cranking and Remo gave it three full spins around, setting off the cluster of squawks inside.

A man in a business suit answered the door.

"Is this the ambassador's residence?" Remo said.

"That is correct." The man's English was precise but had a faint trace of a European accent.

"Well, get him out here. I want to talk to him," Remo said.

"I'm sorry, sir, but he is not at home."

Remo reached out his right hand and caught the man's left earlobe between his thumb and index finger.

"Now where is he?" Remo asked. Through the partially opened door, he could see men lounging in chairs in the hallway. They were armed, because their bodies had the slight off-balance tilt caused by heavy handguns in shoulder holsters.

The man grimaced with pain. "He's at his summer place in Waterbury, sir. Stop, please."

Remo kept squeezing. "Where?"

"His summer place in Waterbury. He will be there for the week."

"Okay," Remo said.

He released the man's ear.

"Is there a message, sir?" the man asked. He rubbed his ear with the palm of his hand.

"No message," Remo said. "I'll see him when he gets back."

The door closed quickly behind Remo as he went back to the cab and hopped inside.

"Drive to the corner, James," he said. He leaned closed to Chiun. "It's all right. He's here."

"How do you know?"

"I didn't squeeze him hard enough to force out the truth," Remo said. "He told me what he was supposed to tell me. And if they're shipping people out to Waterbury, wherever that is, that means he's hiding out here. Particularly when there are a bunch of guys with guns hanging around."

At the corner where the road hung left in a series of steps toward Greater Marlborough Street, Remo and Chiun got out.

Remo gave the driver five American dollars.

"That's about three pounds now," Remo said. "Hold it for twelve hours and at your usual inflation rate, it'll probably be up to five pounds. Hold it a week and you can buy a house."

As he drove away, the driver muttered, "I'll hold it a month and buy a bomb to stick up your blinking bum, smartass Yank."

As Chiun and Remo walked back down the rain-slicked street toward the ambassador's residence, Chiun asked, "Are we anywhere near London Bridge?"

"No."

"Where is it?"

104

"I think it's in Arizona. They sold the thing and somebody moved it to Arizona."

"Did he buy the river too?" asked Chiun.

"Don't be silly. Of course not."

"Why would he buy a bridge and move it to Arizona?" Chiun asked.

"I don't know," Remo said. "Maybe he's got a water problem out there. I don't know."

"I am always amazed by the depth and breadth of the things you do not know," Chiun said.

Remo had an idea. Chiun did not seem interested.

"It's a pretty good idea, Chiun," Remo said.

Chiun said nothing. He looked around the third-floor bedroom, which they had entered by forcing a window after sliding up the outside drainpipe from the sidewalk below.

"This is it," Remo said. "The idea."

Chiun looked at him.

"You ready?" Remo asked.

Chiun sighed.

Remo said, "See, we've got no orders on what to do with this guy except keep him alive. So what we'll do is bundle him up, take him on the plane with us back to the U.S. Then we give him to Smitty and that way nothing can happen to him. What do you think?"

"Even the most subtle languages begin somewhere with a grunt," Chiun said.

But Remo was not listening. He had crossed the bedroom and was peering through a crack in the door.

Outside was a drawing room and a man in shirtsleeves was sitting at a table playing solitaire.

There were five other men in the room. Four of them wore the too-tight-in-the-chest, too-loose-in-the-hips blue business suits of the KGB. They took turns walking to the windows and looking outside, opening the door to the hall and glancing around, checking behind the long drapes in case someone was hiding there. And when one finished making those rounds—windows, door, drapes—another began. Windows, door, drapes. The fifth man in the room stood near the man who was playing cards, emptying the man's almost-empty ashtray, refilling his almost-full drinking glass, shuffling the cards for him after each game.

Remo recognized the seated man as the ambassador. He had golden blond curls that framed his broad forehead and his face had the healthy tan of sun and summer and Remo wondered where he had managed to find either in London. The man wore a tapered shirt that hugged his trim body. Smith had given Remo a brief folder with the photograph and background of Ambassador Semyon Begolov. It had described him as the Casanova of the world's diplomatic corps and Remo could see why.

Begolov was asking the KGB men to play poker with him.

"We cannot play cards with you, Excellency," one of the four KGB men said. "There was that American who came calling for you a little while ago. We must be on the alert lest he return. And someone who is playing at games is not working at his duties for the motherland." He was a grim and smug twerp giving the ambassador a lesson in being a good dedicated Communist.

Begolov played a red ten on a black jack and winked to the man who stood behind him.

"You know, if I'm killed, it'll be the salt mine for all of you. I think I'll commit suicide. I'll shoot myself and drop the gun out the window as I'm falling to the floor. Then they'll blame it on some American CIA assassin and you'll all go to Siberia. I can do it, you know, and get away with it."

The four KGB men looked at him, startled and shocked. Remo shook his head. The KGB had no sense of humor at all.

"Now I can promise you that I will not do that," Begolov said.

"But of course you would not do that," said the KGB stiff.

"I might, though," said Begolov. "Anything is possible. However, if you were to play poker with me, well, then I would be so much in your debt that you would have my promise never to do such a thing."

Remo left the door open a crack and went back to tell Chiun it would be some time before they could spirit Begolov away without KGB interference. Outside, he heard Begolov tell someone, probably the tall, thin-faced valet, to get the poker chips.

It took an hour.

Remo heard the chairs push away from the table.

"Since you men seem to have run out of

money," Begolov said, "I have suddenly become tired. It is time for bed."

"We will stand guard through the night out here, Excellency," the stiff said.

"Please do. I would rather not have you in bed with me."

Remo waited behind the door as Begolov entered the bedroom. He clapped a hand over the man's mouth as the door closed and whispered crisply in the ambassador's ear.

"Don't make a sound," he said. "I'm not going to hurt you. Just listen. I'm from the United States. I know you're in danger and I've been sent to protect you. What we want is for you to sneak out with us and fly to Washington. An assassin'll never track you down there."

He felt Begolov relax slightly.

"Think about it," Remo said. "Here, they might get you any time. Like they did those guys in Rome and Paris. But in Washington? Not a chance. What do you say?"

Begolov mumbled; Remo felt the vibrations against the fingers of his hand.

"No yelling," Remo said. "Just soft talkie-talk."

Begolov nodded and Remo released his mouth slightly.

"It seems an interesting idea," the ambassador said. "Anything would be better than spending much more time with these secret police types."

Remo nodded. He did not look at Chiun who was sitting on Begolov's bed, shaking his head.

"But I couldn't go alone," Begolov said.

"You sure as hell can't take all those guards," Remo said. "I'm not Pan American Airlines."

"Just Andre," said Begolov. "My valet. He is always with me."

Remo thought a moment. "All right. Just Andre."

Chiun shook his head again.

"I'll call him," Begolov said.

Remo opened the door a few inches.

Begolov called out, "Andre, will you come here, please?"

Andre, the tall, thin man, stepped inside the room. He closed the door behind him, saw Chiun on the bed, then turned and saw Begolov standing with Remo.

"This is him," Begolov shouted at the top of his voice. "The American assassin. Help, Andre."

Andre backed off a few steps. Outside the door, Remo could hear the thud of heavy feet running toward the bedroom. Andre reached into his back pocket and drew a pistol. He took careful aim and shot Begolov between the eyes.

Chiun sat on the bedspread, shaking his head from side to side.

Andre pointed the gun at his own chin, but before he could squeeze the trigger, Remo let Begolov's body drop to the floor and had moved over to Andre, covering the hammer of the revolver with his own hand to prevent its firing.

The door burst open and the four KGB men rushed in, guns in hand.

Remo took out two of the guns with a sweeping kick. The others fired. Their slugs hit Andre.

"Crap," said Remo. "Nothing ever goes right. I was saving him."

He let Andre drop and moved in among the four men who spread out into a rough diamond with Remo at the center.

"Chiun, are you going to help or are you just going to sit there?"

"Do not invite me into your catastrophe now," Chiun said. "It is none of my doing."

One of the KGB men turned to cover Chiun with his automatic.

Chiun raised his hands in surrender.

Two others grabbed Remo's arms. The third put the gun to Remo's throat.

"All right, American," the KGB stiff said. "Now we haff you."

"You haff nothing," Remo said. His two hands moved out from his sides where his arms were pinned by the two agents and the backs of his elbows bent and then slammed upward. Two Russian sternums were cracked and the bones driven backwards into two Russian hearts. And as Remo did it, he was falling backward, and the KGB stiff squeezed the trigger, but Remo was not there. He was under the shot and then moving up with a stiff butt of his hand into the soft under-throat of the KGB leader who dropped like a stone.

The man covering Chiun wheeled around and instinctively squeezed the trigger but it was too late because Remo had twisted the gun in on the man himself, and the bullet ripped into his own chest cage.

Remo glared at Chiun.

"A fine lot of help you are."

"I tried to help you before," Chiun said. His arms were folded stubbornly over his chest. "But no. You could not learn anything from the Great Master Ung. So you let the victim invite in the assassin and then you're surprised that he is the assassin. Remo, you are hopeless."

"That's enough carping. And that's also enough of the Great Master Wang and the Greater Master Ung and the Greatest Master of them all, Master Dingdong. No more. I'm done with all that."

There were sounds in the hall.

Chiun was off the bed like a windblown wisp of blue smoke.

"Unless it is your goal to murder the entire KGB," Chiun said, "we should leave."

Remo looked out the window, "The bobbies are already down there."

"Then go up," said Chiun.

With Chiun only a few inches behind him, Remo went out through the window like a pistol shot and gracefully somersaulted up onto the roof, eight feet above the window ledge. The roof was steeply pitched slate, wet and slippery in the foggy London night. They moved across it as surely as if on rails.

They went across four roofs before they came down a fire escape on Wardour Street and Remo hailed a cab to go back to the airport.

Remo sulked in a corner of the cab and Chiun was silent too, as if in commiseration.

"You don't have to be quiet, just because you're feeling sorry for me," Remo said.

"I'm not feeling sorry for you," Chiun said. "I'm thinking."

"About what?" Remo asked.

"What will Ruby screech when you tell her you failed?" Chiun said.

Remo groaned.

CHAPTER NINE

Mrs. Harold W. Smith was happier than she could recall having been in years.

At the start, she had had a moment's doubt. When her husband told her he had hired a new assistant at the sanitarium and then that the assistant was a young woman, well, she worried a little about that, because after all Harold W. Smith was a man and he might be reaching that age when men all seem to go temporarily or permanently crazy.

But the worry had been short-lived. She knew her husband well. And soon, she began to wonder why Harold—even in her mind, it was always Harold, never Harry or Hal—why he had not hired an assistant years before.

Because suddenly, Harold was getting a chance to go out in the afternoons and play golf and he was coming home for dinner for the first time in all his years of running that terrible dull sanitarium, and for the first time in many years, Mrs. Smith had other things to do with her life than meet with other members of the Ladies Aid Society and roll cancer dressings.

She had taken her cookbooks out of the shoe box in the hall closet and had begun again to enjoy working in the kitchen. Her mother had once told her that a well-cooked meal was a performance, but no performance had meaning unless it had an audience. Now, for the first time in years, she had her audience back.

Mrs. Smith was busy now pounding thin strips of veal into paper-thin slices for veal parmigiana. She glanced at the wristwatch Harold her given her as a present thirty years before. He would be home any minute. And she would put a glass of white wine in his hand and sit him in the living room with his slippers and fifteen minutes later she would have on the table a meal fit for a king. Or an emperor.

It had all happened very quickly. Harold W. Smith had been thinking about Remo and Chiun's failure in London. He had been fed the computer printouts of the Associated Press and United Press International wire copy filed on the mass murder at the home of the Russian ambassador in London. And he had been driving mechanically, his mind on Project Omega, rushing remorselessly to its conclusion which might just be the death of the Russian premier and the start of World War III.

Smith stopped at a red light, before turning off the main street in Rye, New York, up into the hill section of town where he lived with his wife in a modest tract house whose value had increased in the ten years he had owned it, from $27,900 to $62,500, and on which he often congratulated himself, it being the only good personal business deal he had ever made in his life.

He wasn't looking and then there was a man in the car, leaning over from the backseat, with a gun stuck in Smith's ribs. He spoke with an accent.

"Drive straight ahead."

Two blocks later, the man directed him to pull to the curb and park. They both got out of the car and into a red Chevrolet Nova where a man with a cowboy hat was sitting behind the wheel.

Smith automatically recorded the car's license number in his memory as they got into the backseat. The man in the cowboy hat looked into the rearview mirror and his eyes met Smith's.

"Doctor Smith?"

Smith nodded.

He recognized Colonel Vassily Karbenko, head of Russia's spy network in the United States, but he decided there would be nothing to be gained, and perhaps much to be lost, by saying anything now.

"Good," said Karbenko. "We have much to talk about." He put the car into drive and pulled smoothly out into the late supper traffic. The man sitting next to Smith kept the gun pushed into Smith's ribs.

She called at twenty after eight.

"Miss Gonzalez," Mrs. Smith said. "The doctor isn't home yet."

Ruby pursed her lips. Smith had left the office an hour ago and told Ruby he was going straight home. Straight home for Harold Smith meant straight home, Ruby knew. It didn't mean stopping for gas, for a newspaper, for a pack of cigarettes, for a drink at the neighborhood saloon. It meant straight home. A nine-minute drive. Eight minutes and forty-five seconds if he was lucky and missed the light on the corner of Desmond and Bagley Streets.

"Oh, I'm sorry, Mrs. Smith. The doctor was called into the city at the last minute," Ruby lied. "He asked me to tell you he's be late. I'm sorry."

"Oh," said Mrs. Smith. The disappointment in her voice struck at Ruby's heart. "Men just have no idea what veal cutlets cost."

"They sure don't, Mrs. Smith. As soon as I hear from him, I'll let you know."

"Thank you, Miss Gonzalez." Mrs. Smith hung up. She was annoyed. The least this Gonzalez girl could have done would be to call before she had gotten the cutlets ready for the oven.

Ruby did not put down the telephone. She called the guardhouse in front of the sanitarium and got the license plate number of the red Chevrolet she had seen loitering across the street.

She punched up the computer console on Smith's desk and fed the license plate number into it. The computer was hooked up through interlocking networks with computer systems all over the country. This time Ruby picked the New York State motor vehicle records connection and waited for a return on the owner of the car.

It took two minutes. The computer sent a message onto the small television-type screen on Smith's desk.

"No record of vehicle registration."

"Sheeit," Ruby mumbled. "Goddamn New York can't do nothin' right." Since she had moved to

Rye to work for Smith, her life had been a continuous series of run-ins with the New York State bureaucracy, typified by her problems in trying to register her white Lincoln Continental in New York. Not only were the state's auto registration fees the highest in the nation but the registration form—which was accomplished in most other states on a single postcard-sized piece of paper—ran to seven separate documents and required a law firm to fill out. Ruby finally surrendered and kept her Virginia plates and if she ever got stopped and got any lip from a state trooper for having an out-of-state registration, she was going to run the sucker down.

She got out the Westchester County telephone book and began rifling through the yellow pages.

She began calling all those service stations listed for Rye, New York.

Ruby had found that people were never suspicious of the stupid, so she turned her accent into deep dripping Alabama.

"Hello. Mah name be Madie Jackson. Ah's tryin' to fahnd me a car ah hits today in a parkin' lot. A red Nova. Ah wanna call the owner and fix up his car for he."

On the twelfth call, she got lucky.

"Yeah, Madie," said a black voice from Cochran's Service. "That be Gruboff's car."

"Who?"

"Igor Gruboff, some funny name like that. He live up on Benjamin Place. He here complainin' all the time. Hey, Madie, what you doin' after you call him?"

"Depends on what ah's offered," Ruby said.

"Ah closes down at 11. Then it's party time."

"Look for me," Ruby said.

"What you be drivin', Madie?"

"A blue deuce and a quarter," Ruby said.

"All raht," said the gas station man. "Hey, Madie, you gonna go see this Gruboff?"

"Ah thought ah just call him."

"Don' let him jive you none. He a tight-ass suckah and he be tryin' to con you outa yo' money."

"Thanks, brother. Ah be careful and ah see you at 'leven."

"Ah'll be waiting. You'll know me. Ah be the handsome one."

"Ah can tell," Ruby said and hung up the telephone.

She found Igor Gruboff's address on Benjamin Place in the telephone directory. On a hunch, she punched it into CURE's computers.

The printout came back that Igor Gruboff, fifty-one, was a communications specialist, working with micro-processing. He and his wife had defected from Russia eighteen years earlier, been granted asylum, and seven years ago had become American citizens. Mrs. Gruboff had died two years earlier. Gruboff was employed at Molly Electronics, which had four government contracts for silicon memory chips used in spacecraft.

Ruby nodded. So much for the defection. Gruboff was still one of them. She remembered the man in the cowboy hat she had seen behind the wheel of the red Nova. Somehow, she doubted that that was Gruboff. She punched in the cow-

118

boy-hat description of the man into the computer and called for a correlation check against known Russian agents in the United States.

The machine responded in less than ten seconds.

"Colonel Vassily Karbenko, cultural attache to the Russian Embassy in Washington, D.C. Forty-eight years old. Given to wearing cowboy clothes. Actual rank, colonel in the KGB. Considered a personal protégé of the Russian premier. In the field, Russia's highest-ranking spy in the United States."

On a sheet of white paper, Ruby printed in large block letters the name and address of Igor Gruboff. She left it on Smith's desk for whoever might find it. In case finding it became necessary.

The cellar of Igor Gruboff's home had been turned into a recreation room by putting ugly knotty pine panels over ugly cinderblock walls.

Harold Smith was directed to a chair by Vassily Karbenko, who dropped his large Stetson on a table, then stood looking at Smith.

Igor Gruboff stood by the steps leading to the kitchen, his hand inside his jacket pocket, holding a revolver. Smith noticed that like almost all foreigners his trousers were too short.

"Might I ask who you are?" Smith said.

"You don't know?" Karbenko said. He hooked his thumbs into his belt loops and leaned back against the table.

"No, I don't," Smith lied. "I don't go to cowboy movies."

Karbenko smiled. "Good," he said. "Very good.

119

But suppose we just leave it at that. That you don't know who I am. What is important is that I know who you are, or, more accurately, who you used to be."

Smith nodded.

"I want to know about Project Omega," Karbenko said.

"I don't know what you're talking about."

"Doctor Smith, let us clear the air," Karbenko said. "Your name is Harold W. Smith. You run Folcroft Sanitarium. Twenty years ago, while working for the Central Intelligence Agency, you devised a program called Project Omega. It was designed to bring about the assassination of certain Russian officials if the United States should lose a nuclear war. Its alleged purpose was to prevent such a war. It succeeded. Then you retired from the service. Through no fault of yours, Project Omega has been triggered. Three Russian ambassadors have been killed. The Russian premier is on the list for extinction. No one knows how to call off Project Omega. Yet, if it is not stopped before the Russian premier is killed, it might well be the first explosion in World War III. I have no reason to believe that you are not a dedicated American patriot who does not want his country, and the world, ravaged by nuclear war. While I represent the other side, my goal is identical to yours. I find it necessary that we talk now to try to determine if there is any way to head off Omega before its damage becomes irrevocable. That is why I am here."

"I told everything I know to officials of my government," Smith said. He folded his arms across his chest.

"So I was told. However, Doctor, I do not believe that the current officials of your government and its CIA could find their feet in their shoes. My government is becoming very nervous. Anything is possible now and I need to know everything."

Smith was silent.

"So let us get right to it, shall we? I have been told by Admiral Stantington that there were four targets for CIA assassins under Project Omega. The ambassadors to Rome, Paris, and London, all of whom are dead now, and the Russian premier. Who picked the targets?"

"I did," Smith said.

"How, twenty years ago, could you pick today's ambassador and premier? I do not understand or believe this," Karbenko said.

"Two of the targets were geographic picks," Smith said. "That is, the envoys to Paris and Rome were to be marked for extinction. The assassins would have operated against whoever turned out to be the ambassadors to those countries."

"I see," said Karbenko. "And the other two? The English ambassador and the premier?"

"I drew up a list of ten young diplomats. I was sure the ambassador to England would be on that list."

"You say you drew up a list of ten diplomats. Do you mean there are nine more diplomats in Russia with assassins trailing them around?"

"That would be correct," Smith said, "except

that they are dormant. They are not in a position to attack because their instructions were to . . . er, dispose of their man only if he was the ambassador to England."

"And the premier? How did you know who would be the premier, here and now, twenty years later?"

"I did not. I selected six candidates," Smith said.

"I find that hard to believe. Twenty years ago, you could have polled the Politburo and their consensus would not have placed our current premier in the six most likely candidates. How did you succeed?"

"I used different standards, perhaps, from those of the Politburo," Smith said.

"And what were those standards?"

"I selected the three most vicious and the three dumbest," Smith said.

Gruboff growled near the staircase but Karbenko laughed.

"Under the age-old theory that either the most brutal or the dumbest will prevail?" Karbenko asked.

"Correct," said Smith. "Never the normal. The brutal or the stupid."

"I will not ask you into which category our current premier falls," said Karbenko.

"I wish you wouldn't," Smith said.

"Who selected the assassins?" asked Karbenko.

"Another CIA man," Smith answered. "Conrad MacCleary. He is dead now."

"And you expect me to believe that you did not know whom he selected?"

"That's right," Smith said. "I didn't approve of MacCleary. I don't think I would want to know who he selected. Or how."

"How? How *might* he select somebody?"

"In MacCleary's case," Smith said, "one could never tell. It might be somebody he hustled at a card game. Or some drinking buddy. Or some woman he made fall in love with him. Somebody with relatives in the United States that he threatened. Or just somebody he bribed."

"How could this MacCleary have done this without leaving a record for anyone in the CIA?"

"Because those were his instructions," Smith said. "From President Eisenhower, through me. Of course, no one knew that the project would someday be triggered."

Karbenko nodded, and then carefully and slowly brought Smith back over the same ground.

He was not interested in what this Doctor Smith thought he knew or didn't know. He wanted to find out what Smith actually knew and sometimes the two things were different. Perhaps MacCleary had dropped a name one night, mentioned some incident, let fall a hint. Careful interrogation took time and Colonel Vassily Karbenko was ready to use as much time as was necessary.

He reflected grimly that he had nothing else on his schedule.

Except perhaps World War III.

Ruby Jackson Gonzalez parked her white Lincoln Continental half a block down Benjamin Place from Igor Gruboff's house.

She rooted around in the trunk for a moment

and found a Gideon Bible wedged in behind the spare tire. The Bible was her mother's. When Ruby used to take her for Sunday drives, the old lady would read the Bible and lecture Ruby on driving too fast.

She had finally stopped when Ruby installed a giant CB radio for her mother to play with on those Sunday drives. She no longer cared how fast Ruby drove.

Ruby's CB handle was "Down Home." Her mother, who wore her hair inside a bandana, smoked a corncob pipe and never had anything on her feet but bedroom slippers, called herself "Midnight Lace."

Ruby rang the doorbell of the Gruboff house. There was no answer. She rang the bell again, four times, staccato. When there was still no answer, she leaned on the bell steadily.

In the basement where the doorbell rang, Karbenko stared angrily at it, then ordered Gruboff, "Go answer that. Wait. Leave me your gun."

The burly Russian gave Karbenko his pistol. Karbenko placed it on the table behind him, with a glance at Smith that was shared commiseration, the acknowledgment by one professional to another that sometimes one had to do tasteless things in their business.

Gruboff plodded up the steps. The doorbell kept ringing. He pulled the door open and saw a young black woman standing there.

She raised her right index finger in the air like an eighteenth-century orator making a point. She waved the Gideon Bible in her left hand.

" 'By this, all will know that you are among my

disciples if you have love among yourselves,' " she said.

"Huh?" said Gruboff.

"I am here to give you a free gift," Ruby said. She tried to look past Gruboff down the hallway of his house but his bulky body filled the doorway and sealed off her view.

"I don't want any," Gruboff said gutturally. He started to close the door.

"Wait," said Ruby. " 'A gift is as a precious stone in the eyes of him that hath it; whithersoever it turneth, it prospereth.' Proverbs."

"I told you, I don't want none," Gruboff said.

"I want no money," Ruby said. "I'm going to give you this Bible. And I'm going to give you a copy of our free twice-monthly magazine, the *Watchword*. And then you'll get a copy every two weeks and you'll get a personal visit from me every five days, rain or shine, so we can stand out here on your porch and talk about the Bible." Under her breath, she mumbled "and you can really get to hate me."

"I'm an atheist," said Gruboff. "I don't want your Bible."

"An atheist!" Ruby said, as if proclaiming a victory. " 'The fool hath said in his heart, there is no God.' Psalms."

"Aaaaaah," snarled Gruboff.

"Try this one," said Ruby. " 'We speak that we do know and testify that we have seen; and ye receive not our witness.' John, Three-Eleven."

"Go away, lady."

"You're not interested in the free Bible?"

"No."

"Not in our free bi-monthly magazine, the *Watchword*?"

"No," said Gruboff.

"Not in my visiting you every five days to talk about the scriptures? I generally call when you're in the shower."

"No," said Gruboff.

"All right," said Ruby. She reached into her purse. "One last word."

"Just one," said Gruboff.

"This is from Acts. Eight-eighteen," Ruby said. " 'Give me also this authority that anyone upon whom I lay my hands may receive the holy spirit.' "

She smiled at Gruboff. "Here's yours," she said. She pulled the revolver from her purse, swung it and cracked Gruboff on the side of the skull. He staggered back from the doorway. "Move on out, honkey," Ruby said.

She followed him inside and closed the door, and waited for his eyes to clear.

"Where is he?" she asked. She pointed the gun at Gruboff, holding it expertly low and close to her hip so no wild swing of hand or foot could dislodge it before she could fire.

"Where is who?" said Gruboff, groggily.

"That's one," said Ruby. She pulled back the slide on the automatic. The locking sound was brittle hard in the still hallway. "Try for two? Where is he?"

Gruboff looked at her, then at the gun.

"This is a .22 caliber Ruger semi-automatic, the weakest handgun in the world," Ruby said. "The cartridges are five years old and the gun may be rusty. Even if I hit you right between the eyes, I might not be able to stop you. Now what you have to ask yourself is, do you think I'll get lucky?"

She was smiling at Gruboff but there was no humor in the smile and Gruboff looked at the gun again, then grunted, "Downstairs."

"Lead the way. No tricks."

Gruboff went down the steps, Ruby close behind him. In the cellar, Karbenko looked up and saw the anguished look on his underling's face. He reached behind him for the revolver on the table.

Gruboff took a step into the cellar and Ruby stood behind him at the bottom of the steps, her gun trained on Karbenko.

The tall Russian smiled at her.

"Doctor Smith, who is this lovely lady to the rescue?" he asked.

"My administrative assistant," Smith said.

"You be all right, Doctor?" Ruby asked.

"Yes."

"Okay. You, Roy Rogers. Get over there on the couch. You too, gorilla." She waved with the gun.

Gruboff moved in front of her and, as he did, Colonel Karbenko snatched the gun from the table behind him and sprinted the one step toward Smith where he stood behind the CURE director and put the barrel of the gun against Smith's temple.

"Sheeit," said Ruby.

"Put down your weapon, little lady," said Karbenko.

Stubbornly, Ruby held the weapon on Karbenko for a moment. Then slowly her hand wavered and dropped. Gruboff stepped over and yanked the automatic from her hand.

He raised his other hand to punch her but was stopped by a barked command from Karbenko.

"None of that, Igor," he said.

Igor glared at Ruby with hatred. There was a large purplish bruise blossoming on the side of his face where Ruby had hit him.

"I know you not sell Bible," he said to her.

"Three more minutes and I coulda sold you your own car, dummy," Ruby said.

"Over here," Karbenko said. He motioned Ruby to a seat on the couch next to Smith.

"Now, Doctor," Karbenko said, "everything grows vastly more complicated. I believed what you told me about Project Omega. But now something tells me that everything is not quite right."

"Why?" Smith asked.

"Because I know very few sanitarium directors whose administrative assistants carry automatics."

"If you lived in my neighborhood, you'd carry a submachine gun," Ruby said.

Karbenko smiled. "Clever, child. But it will not do."

He looked at Smith. "I was willing to risk my contact with you," he said. "I had even made preparations for Igor here to return to Russia since his cover was so obviously blown by helping me pick you up. But now, not just you . . . this girl, too. You have put me in a very awkward situation, Doctor Smith."

"You have my deepest sympathy," Smith said.

Karbenko picked the revolver up from the table and hefted it in his hand.

"You know what I must do, don't you?"

Another voice came into the cellar.

"No. What must you do?"

Ruby turned. It was Remo. He was standing at the foot of the stairs alongside Igor. Chiun was next to him. Igor turned, a dumbfounded look on his face, because he had not heard them come down the stairs.

He pointed the automatic at Remo and his finger began to squeeze on the trigger. Remo clutched Igor's wrist. His fingers searched out a bundle of nerves on the bottom side of the wrist. Igor's trigger finger could squeeze no more.

"Who's in charge here?" Remo asked.

"I am," Karbenko said coldly.

Remo looked at Igor. "Sorry, Kong. But you're just baggage." He released Igor's wrist. Igor continued squeezing the trigger. Ruby was surprised that the tired old .22 automatic went off. Igor was even more surprised, because when it fired, the gun was pointing up into Igor's chin. The bullet ran through the soft flesh and buried itself in his brain. Igor dropped.

"I thought you never get here," Ruby screeched.

"Shut up, you," said Remo, "or I'm leaving. You're next, Tex."

Karbenko aimed the pistol at Remo.

"Who are these people, Smith?" he said.

"Two more of my administrative assistants," Smith said. "Remo, don't kill him."

"Hold, hold," said Chiun. "What is this? *Who* is an administrative assistant?"

"Why not kill him?" Remo asked Smith. "Everybody knows the only good cowboy is a dead cowboy."

Chiun was jumping up and down. "An administrative assistant? Who? Not me. Who then? What did you mean by that, Emperor Smith?"

"Don't kill him," Smith repeated to Remo. "We need Colonel Karbenko."

When he heard Smith speak his name, Karbenko's eyes shifted slightly toward the thin balding doctor, sitting on the couch. Just a tiny shift, done and over in a fraction of a second. Then he looked back toward the young American and the old Oriental, but they were not there. He felt the gun being snatched from his hand by the Oriental and the American, the one called Remo, was propelling him backward into a chair.

"Sit down and behave yourself," Remo said.

"I don't seem to have much choice, pardner," Karbenko said.

"Smile when you call me that," Remo said.

"Who is an administrative assistant?" demanded Chiun.

CHAPTER TEN

It was all decided very swiftly.

Smith's plan was simple.

It was impossible, he said, for the Russians to protect their premier from an assassin who might be anybody, anywhere around him. But there was one way to save the premier.

Bring him to America. Alone. Without an entourage.

And then if he were murdered, America would have to take the blame in the eyes of the world and Russia's leadership would be justified in doing what it felt it had to do.

"It is risky," Karbenko said.

"It is risky for us too," Smith said. "But at least it has a chance of success. Leaving your premier in Russia is not risky at all. He will be dead in no more than a few days."

"What makes you think I can convince him?" Karbenko said.

"I know more about you, Colonel, than you think," Smith said. "The premier regards you as a son. He will listen to your recommendation."

Karbenko nodded. "Yes, he will."

"Then make it," Smith urged. "And then we

can join forces in protecting the premier here until the assassin is uncovered."

Karbenko's eyes crinkled as he thought.

"Okay, pardner. You got a deal," he said.

"Whoopee ti-yi-yo," Remo said.

"He must have meant you when he said administrative assistant," Chiun said to Remo.

CHAPTER ELEVEN

The carpet was a gold woolen pile, deep enough to drop a dime into and lose sight of the coin. The desk was a giant oaken box. It had once been used by Stalin. When Khrushchev had come into power and attacked Stalin's reputation, the desk had been put into the Kremlin basement along with the other trash.

But then, a few years later, when he, too, was safely out of office, Khrushchev's own reputation had been attacked. So the teak desk he had bought for the premier's office was put into the basement and Stalin's desk dragged out, refinished, polished, and put back in the sixth-floor office.

But the rug that Khruschev had installed was too new and the Stalin rug too old and worn and threadbare to be reinstalled, so the gold rug was left on the floor.

Sometimes the new premier envied America. The White House, he was told, still had a Lincoln bed. There were signs all over American announcing where George Washington had slept. Presidents' homes were national shrines. In

America, heroes remained heroes and history remained history.

Not so in the Kremlin. The Kremlin even had a man assigned to its custodial department whose sole job was to continue shifting around furniture whenever the Kremlin decided to change its reading of past history.

The current premier had decided in his first day in office never to buy furniture for it. He would use whatever was left over and was politically reliable, because he regarded it as a waste of time to buy desks and chairs and tables, knowing that in a couple of years after his demise or disposal, they would probably wind up in the Kremlin cellar too as his own successor began to rewrite history.

The only thing in the office that was pure was the globe. It had once belonged to Lenin. Everybody liked Lenin.

The premier was reaching for the telephone when his office door opened and a general whose green uniform was festooned with a chestful of medals and ribbons walked in. He led a contingent of seven men.

The premier looked up, startled. The general had not knocked. The premier slid his chair back ready to dive under the desk, in case bullets started flying.

"General Arkov," the premier said. "What brings you here in such a hurry?"

"Quick, men," the general said. "Check everything."

This is it, the premier thought. Someone had mounted a coup against him and in a moment, he would have a bullet in the brain, the personal gift of General Arkov, head of the KGB.

The seven men with Arkov began scurrying about the office. Two went into the bathroom. One dropped to the rug and began looking under the chairs and sofa. Another crawled under the premier's desk. Two had electronic devices and they scanned the walls and electrical switches.

General Arkov stood in the doorway, watching his men. After a few minutes, they all returned to stand in front of him, shaking their heads.

"All right," Arkov said. "Take positions." The men spread out around the room and Arkov looked, for the first time, at the premier.

Surprised that he was still alive, and thus emboldened, the premier's voice was sharp.

"Now I suppose you will tell me what this is all about?" he said.

"Semyon Begolov is dead. An assassin got him in London, and four of our men assigned to protect him."

"Dead? Who?"

"His valet."

"Andre something? I remember him," the premier said. "He seemed like a quiet enough sort."

"He was. Until last night when he put a bullet into Begolov's head. That is why we are here."

"To put a bullet into my head?" the premier said, and as soon as he had said it, he wished he hadn't. Arkov's eyes narrowed as if a joke were a sign of weakness and he must forever after keep a close watch on the premier.

"No, premier. To make sure that no assassin tries to do the same to you."

The premier looked around the office at the seven KGB men. They stood watching him, looking ill at ease, shifting their weight from foot to foot.

"And I am supposed to work like this?" the premier said.

"I am sorry but we have no alternative. We must protect you the best way we can."

"Protect me from the outside office."

"No." The answer was flat and formal and final.

The premier shrugged. His telephone rang. His hand reached for the telephone but before he could get to it, one of the KGB men had intercepted him. The man picked up the telephone himself, cautiously, before speaking into it.

"There are many devices, Premier," General Arkov explained. "A sound signal could come over a telephone that could paralyze you. A needle might have been inserted into the earpiece of your receiver, so it could puncture your brain when you talk on the phone."

"I think somebody punctured your brain," the premier grumbled. He looked up angrily at the KGB agent who had finished inspecting the telephone and handed it to him.

It was the premier's secretary asking if he wanted coffee.

"No. Vodka," he growled. "A big glass. With ice."

"So early in the day?" she said.

"You too?" he asked. "Better yet, bring me a bottle."

"You know what the doctor said, sir."

"And you know what I said. A bottle and a glass. Skip the ice."

That there was no working in the office became clear in only minutes. Every time the telephone rang, one of the agents intercepted the call. Every time the intercom buzzed, the agent with the small electronic-box scanned it before allowing him to answer. His vodka was taste-tested before he was allowed any. He poured twice the size drink he had planned.

When his newspapers arrived, another agent went through each page first for hidden bombs and then General Arkov and they debated on whether the ink of the paper itself might be poisoned and whether it should be sent out for laboratory analysis.

The premier resolved the problem for them. He jerked the paper from Arkov's hands.

"Give me that newspaper," he said. He walked toward the door to his private bathroom.

"Where are you going?" Arkov said.

"To the bathroom, where do you think?"

"Just a moment," Arkov said. "Men."

Two men scurried into the bathroom. They closed the door behind them. The premier heard the faucet running. He heard the medicine cabinet being opened and closed. He heard the toilet flush. He heard the shower run and then the bath water. He heard the toilet flush again.

He rocked back and forth from foot to foot, waiting.

The medicine cabinet again. The toilet for a third time.

"Dammit, Arkov," he roared. "I've got to go."

"Just a moment, sir," Arkov said.

"Another moment and you're going to have to send out to get me new pants."

The two KGB men left the bathroom and the premier shoved them aside, hurrying inside.

He read the newspaper carefully, from front to back. Stubbornly, he rubbed his fingertips over the ink of the pages and, when he was done, his fingers were stained black with the oily gum of the ink.

He washed his hands.

"Did you check the soap to see if it's poisoned?" he yelled out.

"No," called back Arkov. The premier heard men scurrying toward the bathroom door. He leaned over and locked it.

"Good," he said.

When he was done washing his hands, he dropped the newspaper into the waste basket in the bathroom and went outside. Three agents were dismantling the overhead light.

"Looking for a death ray gun, I suppose," the premier said.

"Or a bomb," Arkov said.

"Idiot. Did it ever occur to you that our three ambassadors have been killed by humans? By people close to them? Why should I be different? Why should I be killed by a device or a machine?"

"I cannot take chances, Excellency," the general said.

"And I can't take this nonsense. I'm going home. Call me when the proletariat throws off its chains. Or you find an assassin lurking in my desk drawer or my inkwell. Whichever comes first."

General Arkov insisted upon riding in the back seat of the limousine with the premier. The KGB chief kept his holster unbuttoned and his right hand on the butt of his gun, and a watchful eye on the man who had been the premier's driver for almost ten years.

Three KGB men rode in a car in front of the premier and four more in a car following them. At Arkov's direction, the road leading out of Moscow had been sealed to all other traffic and the premier did not see another moving car during the entire thirty-minute drive to the small house in the countryside outside Moscow.

The large wall surrounding the small house was a new addition, but the rest of the house was much as it had been when the premier was young and still working his way up through the Communist Party ranks, when it had been him and Nina, just him and Nina, and a hope that he would survive the Stalin purges and the Khrushchev counter-purges and the continuous plotting in the KGB and the Army.

He had survived them all. And now he led. There were party congresses and committees and the secret police and the military and the more-bread-and-butter factions, all the groups who were trying to impress on Mother Russia their own blueprint for the future. But there was only one premier and his hand was the hand on the nuclear button.

Odd that he should think of that, he realized. With America laying back all over the world after it declined to fight for victory in Vietnam, the Russian program for the world was proceeding on schedule. Black Africa was slowly coming under Communist control. All the Americans had left in Africa was South Africa and they seemed intent upon destroying that.

Every time he read an American press report condemning South Africa, he had to stifle a laugh. The previous week, he had read one respected paper lamenting the injustice that in South Africa, only whites could vote. Apparently it had never occurred to them that in the rest of Africa, nobody could vote.

But that was a picture of America lying down and dying, and this was something different. There were assassins about, assassins bought and paid for in some mysterious way by America twenty years earlier, and three ambassadors had been killed and he was the next target.

Would he start a nuclear war to save his own life? The premier wondered. No matter how powerful a man was, no matter what responsibilities he had to history and to his homeland, he never came easily to the idea of death. At the advice of his secretariat, the premier had not yet accused the United States publicly of the embassy murders. It would be an easy matter to get most of the world to believe that the U.S. had plotted and carried them out. All the American newspapers would believe the story. And while that might serve Russia's short-term interests, it would also point out, even to the stupid, that the United States had somehow infiltrated the personal staffs of three of the Soviet's top diplomats.

And that did not at all look like the picture of a country playing dead. It would look like a CIA on the move and he was not sure he wanted to encourage that picture. The Third World followed power.

The KGB men made him wait in the car while they went inside and searched the house and a few minutes later when he was allowed to enter, he was met inside the door by Nina.

The premier's wife was a dozen years younger than he was. She had been beautiful, but now, in her early fifties, her legs were blooming into telephone poles and her hips into a hassock. But her face was still vibrant and pretty with the peasant shrewdness in it that she had always had. American politicians' wives always seemed to get thinner as their husbands got more successful. He wondered why Russian wives tended to imitate haystacks, but he had no chance to ponder the question because Nina was stamping her sizable foot and demanding, "Who are these lunatics and what are they doing in my house?"

"Security, dear," he said.

"Well, your precious security has just destroyed a cake I have been baking for over an hour. It will be a lump of lead now."

"Talk to General Arkov about it, Nina. He is in charge of complaints today. He has ignored all mine; maybe you'll be luckier."

He began to walk into the kitchen but was stopped by one of the agents who went inside, checked it all first, finishing up his inspection by sticking his head into the refrigerator, apparently to make sure no clever American assassin, disguised as an ear of corn, was hiding in there.

The premier lost his temper. Finally it was decided that he and Nina could be alone in the kitchen. General Arkov would guard the door to the rest of the house. Two agents would stand outside the door leading to the rear yard and the other five agents would stand outside each of the windows, to make sure there was no attack through the windows.

"Fine," said the premier.

"Yes," said Arkov. "One thing."

"What?"

"Keep your heads down."

Nina poured the premier a glass of vodka and herself a glass of white wine, then sat facing him across the kitchen table.

"This is bad," she said.

He shrugged. "Three ambassadors of ours have been killed. I am supposed to be next."

"Who is supposed to kill you?"

"No one knows. A secret American spy."

She clinked glasses with him and he drank deeply from his water glass.

"It is bad," she said.

"Things have been bad before," he said. He slumped back in the chair and looked around the kitchen. "Things were bad when we bought this house. We did not know if we would live or die. I lost my place in the Politburo in one of the purges. Still you managed to make do."

"We always did."

"No," he corrected. "You always did." He reached across the table and touched her hand.

142

"Without a job, you fed us. When I had no money, somehow you furnished this house and made it home for us. When I had no prospects, you made sure that I always wore new clothes and shiny shoes."

"So what did you expect?" Nina asked with a smile that illuminated her face and showed off her once-upon-a-time beauty. "Some kind of American wife that if you want a piece of bread toasted, you have to go out and buy her two new machines? And a lifetime membership in cooking school?"

"No. You are not that," the premier said. "You could always make do. You even had meat on the table when no one else had meat. How do you do it?"

"I'm really the Grand Duchess Anastasia in disguise and I pawned the czar's jewels," she said.

"You couldn't be Anastasia," he said.

"Why not?"

"You're too good a Communist. Besides, you're beautiful and Anastasia looked like the bottom of a boot."

She was about to answer when the telephone on the wall, next to the oven, rang. The premier reached a lazy hand for it but General Arkov burst into the room and took the telephone himself. He inspected the instrument and held the receiver to his ear for a moment, while the premier saw the look of disgust on Nina's face and tried to stop himself from laughing. Finally, Arkov handed him the telephone.

"It's Colonel Karbenko," he said. "His call is

143

being scrambled at both ends and transferred here from your office. You can speak freely."

"Thank you, Arkov," the premier said. "Hello, Vassily, how are you? How are the cattle when you're riding the range?"

The premier listened for a moment, then said, "Don't tell me you're worried, too, Vassily."

He held the telephone away from his ear so that Nina could hear the young spy's voice from America.

"Yes, Comrade. But I think I have a way to insure your safety and . . ."

"And?"

"And if that fails, it will solve our political problem of attacking the Americans."

"What is it, Vassily? Anything is better than having these KGB men inside my hat." General Arkov winced and the premier smiled. Although Arkov was Karbenko's superior in the KGB, Karbenko had much greater political support among the country's top leaders, because of his friendship with the premier, and while Arkov could dislike him, he could do very little else.

"This is the idea, Premier. Do not put the blame for the deaths of these ambassadors on the Americans. Instead, announce that you are coming to America immediately to discuss the killings with the American President. That puts the blame on them without putting the blame on them."

"And what does that have to do with my safety?" the premier asked.

"It is simple, sir. You will come alone. It would seem that the CIA assassin, whoever he might be, is someone close to you. So you come alone. The assassin does not accompany you. You can spend time in America while we track down the assassin."

"And suppose I am . . . what do you cowboys say, rubbed out in America?"

"That's gangsters, premier, not cowboys. But if you're gunned down, then America clearly bears the responsibility for it and our government will do whatever it has to do. But there is much less chance of that happening here than there. Even in your own house, you might not be safe."

"I know it," the premier said. "I expect Arkov's men to come in any minute and start chewing on my shoes. Come alone, you said?"

"Yes, sir."

"What about Arkov?"

"Alone, Comrade," Karbenko insisted.

"I think you're right," the premier said. "I think it's a marvelous idea. I will see you very soon."

He hung up the telephone. "You will be happy to learn, Arkov, that I am going to America to try to flee this assassin."

"The United States?" Arkov said. "You will be a target there for every lunatic."

"I will take my chances. I am going to America."

"I will get ready," Arkov said.

"No, General. I am going alone."

Arkov opened his mouth to argue. The premier's brows dropped, and his expression frosted over, and the KGB chief stopped.

The premier waited until he left the kitchen,

the strut gone from his walk, his shoulders slumping.

Then he asked Nina, "Well, what do you think?"

"I think you're making a mistake," she said.

"You too? You don't want me to go?"

"No. I think America is the safest place for you."

"Then what's the mistake?"

"You said you were going alone," Nina said. "That's the mistake. I'm going with you."

CHAPTER TWELVE

Remo and Chiun waited in an office just outside Smith's office and Ruby Gonzalez watched them as if she expected them to try to steal her jar of rubber cement.

"She makes you feel wanted, doesn't she?" Remo asked.

"It will be a happy day in my life," said Chiun, "when you two present me with a child. Then I will no longer have to associate with either of you."

"Hah!" Ruby said.

"Fat chance," Remo said.

"And then I will bring him up correctly as befits a new Master of Sinanju," said Chiun, ignoring them. "I have gone as far as I can with you."

"Never gonna happen," Ruby said.

"Only because I don't want it to happen," Remo said. "If I wanted it to happen, it'd happen. You can count on that." He glared at Ruby.

"You talk a lot of mess," Ruby said.

"Yeah?" said Remo. "I want you to know that I've got twenty-seven separate steps that I follow to bring a woman to ecstasy. They never fail."

147

"You couldn't remember twenty-seven steps," Ruby said.

"Don't say anything now you're going to regret later," Remo said.

"I will pay one thousand gold pieces for a healthy male child," Chiun announced.

"Each?" asked Ruby.

"Each what?" said Chiun.

"One thousand to me and one thousand to him?"

"No. One thousand total," Chiun said. "Do you think I'm made of gold pieces?"

"Not enough," Ruby said. "Five hundred ain't enough to pay me for my sacrifice."

"No, hah?" said Remo. "Sacrifice, hah? All right. You can have my five hundred gold pieces."

"Then we have a deal," Chiun said.

"I'll think about it," said Ruby.

"I won't," said Remo. "I will not sell my body for mere gold."

"Be quiet, white thing," Chiun said. "This does not concern you."

"What kind of gold pieces?" Ruby suddenly asked, her voice coldly suspicious.

"Nice little ones," Chiun said.

"I want Krugerrands," Ruby said.

"Have you no shame?" said Remo. "Supporting the racist regime of South Africa?"

"Listen, honey, when you talking currency, South Africa be good," Ruby said. "That Krugerrand, that's better than dollars."

The buzzer rang on Ruby's desk. She answered it, then nodded to Remo and Chiun.

"Doctor Smith wants you now."

"He can wait," Chiun said. "This is important."

"He's trying to stop World War III, Chiun," said Remo. "That's important, too."

Chiun dismissed World War III with a wave of his hand. "One thousand Krugerrands to you," he told Ruby. "And you give me his healthy male child."

"Chiun, dammit. That's like a hundred and sixty thousand dollars," Remo said.

"A hundred and seventy-one this morning," Ruby said.

Remo glared at her. "You can buy the whole spawn of some cities for that," he said.

"I know what I want," Chiun said. "We have an agreement?" he pressed at Ruby.

"I got to think about it," she said. "I ain't givin' it up cheap."

Inside his office, Smith was drumming the fingers of both hands on top of his desk. He told Remo and Chiun, "I have spoken to Colonel Karbenko. The Russian premier is arriving this afternoon at Dulles Airport in Washington. Four-fifteen."

"Good," said Chiun. "We will make his death a lesson for all those everywhere who would dare to trifle with this glorious country of the Constitution, Emperor."

Smith shook his head. "No, no, no, no."

He looked at Remo for help. Remo looked out the window.

"I want you both to make sure nothing happens to him while he's here," Smith said. "Until this missing assassin can be turned up."

"All right," Remo said.

"Of course, mighty Emperor," said Chiun. "Your friends are our friends."

"Karbenko is meeting him at the airport," Smith said.

"He knows we're coming?" asked Remo.

"Not exactly."

"How not exactly?" Remo said.

"He wouldn't hear of having any American personnel involved. He wants to do it on his own."

"Very wise," Chiun said.

"He runs a risk of losing the man," Smith said. "But it's a matter of pride with him."

"Very foolish," Chiun said.

"We'll keep him alive," Remo said. "That's it?"

Smith looked at him for a moment, then turned slowly in his chair to look out the one-way windows toward Long Island Sound. "That's it. For now."

Remo had heard those "for nows" before. He stared at Smith's back. The CURE director continued looking out the window.

Outside Folcroft, Chiun said to Remo, "I do not understand this. Russia is your country's enemy, correct?"

"Yes."

"Then why are we saving the head of all the Russias? Why do we not kill him and install our own man on their throne?"

"Chiun," Remo said decisively. "Who knows?"

Admiral Wingate Stantington was walking around the perimeter of his office. The clicking sound of the pedometer on his hip gave him a sense of satisfaction. It was the first time he had felt reasonably good since he had been taken out of his office in a Hefty bag.

Not that he had forgotten that. He never would. And he would get even, he vowed. With the dark-eyed American. With the old Oriental. That black woman who set it all up. His own secretary who allowed it to happen.

He would fix them all. In due time.

It probably had been easier in the old days. He could have just unleashed a CIA hit team, given them their targets and told them to do it. And afterwards, they would be whisked out of the country, set to work in a foreign mission somewhere, and that would be that.

It was different now. Try to find somebody who'd do a little dirty work without worrying all the time about being arrested and indicted. Try to find one who could do it without writing a book about it later on.

When it came time to write his book, he'd let them know what he thought. All of them.

When his private telephone line rang, it was the President telling him that the premier of Russia was arriving that afternoon.

"He can't," Stantington said.

"Why not, Cap?" the President asked.

"We haven't had a chance to put together any kind of security arrangements," Stantington said.

"That's not your concern. I'm just alerting you so you know what's happening in case you hear anything later."

Stantington depressed the button on his telephone tape recorder.

"Officially, Mister President, I have to advise you that I am against this entire idea. I think it is needlessly risky, fraught with peril, and ill-advised."

"I have received and noted your opinion," the President said with chill in his voice as he hung up.

All right, Stantington thought. He was on record. When things went wrong, as they were bound to later, he could tell any Congressional committee with a clear mind and heart that he had advised the President against this course of action. And he had it on tape. He'd be damned if he'd be arrested and indicted for somebody else's mistake.

Stantington sat heavily behind his desk and sighed. But was that enough? Was it enough that he had protected his ass?

He thought about that for no more than thirty seconds and reached his decision.

Yes, it was. There was nothing more important than surviving. The man who had the job before him could languish in a prison chowline. The President could bumble and blunder about. But Admiral Wingate Stantington was going to be as clean as a hound's tooth, and perhaps someday, when they were looking around for viable, clean candidates for offices like President, Wingate Stantington would stand out like a silver dollar atop a pile of pennies.

He leaned back in the chair as he had an idea. He might be able to help that process along—particularly if he was the man who prevented World War III and saved the Russian premier's life in the bargain.

The killings of the three ambassadors had been done by people close to the targets. Now it was Vassily Karbenko's idea to bring the premier to America and Karbenko, it was well known, was like a son to the premier.

Karbenko might fool some others, but could there be any doubt that he was bringing the premier to America so that he would be within the range of Karbenko's own guns?

Stantington was sure of it. Karbenko was the assassin and the President was playing into Karbenko's hands by allowing the Russian premier's visit.

"Get me the files on Colonel Karbenko," Stantington barked into his telephone.

As he waited, he thought about it, and the more he thought, the more sure he was. It was Karbenko. Of course. He felt good about the decision. He felt like a real spy.

The buzzer rang.

"Yes?" he said.

"Sorry, sir, there are no files on Colonel Karbenko."

"No files? Why not?"

"They were probably stolen yesterday afternoon."

"Yesterday? What was yesterday?"

"Don't you remember, sir? You proclaimed it Meet-Your-CIA Day. An open house. We had thousands of people here. Somebody must have taken the files."

Stantington slammed the telephone back on its base. It didn't matter. He was still going to save the Russian premier.

Dulles International Airport was cleverly located so far out of Washington, D.C., that most people couldn't afford the taxi ride to the city and had to take a bus. The smart ones packed a lunch.

The Russian premier and his wife, Nina, arrived quietly in a leased British plane that had picked them up at an airfield in Yugoslavia where they had transferred from a Russian Aeroflot plane.

Colonel Karbenko had made the arrangements. He had to choose among British, French, Italian, and American planes for the last leg of the journey. He had rejected the Italian plane because it might get lost, the French because he knew what French airport mechanics were like, once having lived in Paris. Left to choose between a British aircraft and an American, he picked the British, because, like the Americans, they were competent, and unlike the Americans, the pilot would not immediately sit down to write a book entitled, *Mystery Passenger: A Journey Into Tomorrow.*

Karbenko had an unobtrusive green Chevrolet Caprice parked next to the plane. He went into the plane's passenger compartment, and a moment later, came down the steps followed by the premier and Nina.

The premier was wearing dark sunglasses with a straw hat pulled down over his face. His wife had on a red wig and blue tinted glasses. She wore a two-piece brown suit, so formless that it looked as if it had originally been fitted to a refrigerator.

"We speak the English," the premier said. "That way, nobody know we not Americans."

Karbenko led them across the tarmac of the runway toward his car. He glanced up and noticed Remo and Chiun standing there.

"Good work," said Remo.

"How'd you get here?" Karbenko asked.

"Hail, mighty premier of all the Russias," said Chiun.

"Who is this?" asked the premier.

"I don't exactly know," Karbenko said.

"I am not an administrative assistant," Chiun said. "Hail again."

"Thank you," the premier said. "It is a great pleasure to be here among my American friends."

"I am not an American," Chiun said.

"But I am," Remo said.

"Forget him," Chiun said to the premier.

"What are you doing here?" Karbenko repeated.

"Just making sure," Remo said, "that everything goes right."

CHAPTER THIRTEEN

Two cars followed them as they drove away from the British jetliner. There were four men in each of the cars, and when Vassily Karbenko saw them, he grunted softly and tromped down on the gas pedal of the Chevrolet Caprice.

The car was speeding down an unused runway at the airport, toward an emergency exit onto the highway that surrounded the field. As Karbenko's car sped up, the two other cars separated and increased their speed also, moving up on either side of the premier's car.

The premier seemed oblivious to the chase. His neck was craned and he was looking out across the broad network of runways and hangers at the scores of commercial jetliners. His wife, though, saw the two following cars. She looked toward Karbenko.

"Are they your men, Vassily?" she asked.

"No."

The two cars had pulled up even with Karbenko now. The occupants looked like Americans, Remo thought. The cars started to pull ahead.

"They're going to nose in and nip you between them," Remo said.

"I know," said Karbenko.

The car on the right had its driver's window open.

Remo rolled down his window.

"Vassily," he said. "You stomp on that gas pedal and swerve in close to this car."

"What for?"

"Just do it," Remo said. "When I tell you." Remo raised himself up in the seat, and put his left hand on the door of his car. The car was about two feet in front of them.

"Now," Remo yelled. Karbenko pressed down heavy on the accelerator. The big powerful car surged forward and as it came alongside the car on the right, Karbenko swung the wheel so that only a few inches separated the two cars. At that moment, Remo leaned out his open window. His hands flashed into the car alongside them. Karbenko heard a cracking noise. He glanced to his right, in time to see Remo sinking back into his seat, the steering wheel from the other car in his hands. Beyond Remo, the driver of the other car looked as if he had gone into shock. His face was contorted and his hands waved futilely as he sought some way to steer the car, ripping along the runway at almost 80 miles an hour.

"Get out of here," Remo said. Karbenko powered the Chevrolet forward, just as the driver of the car to their right hit the brakes. But his wheels were not straight and the sudden braking action spun the car sideways and its 80-mile-an-hour forward momentum turned the car over on its side. As Karbenko watched in the rearview mirror, he saw the car roll over three times and then, upside down, skid into the second chase car, knocking it out of control and into a flat grassy field next to the runway, where the driver finally muscled it to a stop.

The four men got out of the car and were running back to free the occupants of the overturned car, when Karbenko pulled onto a narrow gravel road, slowed down, and turned sharply into the line of afternoon traffic.

"Vassily," the premier said. "Don't drive so fast. It makes me nervous."

"No, sir," Karbenko said. He grinned at Remo, who shrugged his shoulders.

"Any idea who that was?" Remo asked.

"Yes," Karbenko said. "I know who it was."

Karbenko had rented three rooms in the name of the Earp family at an eight-dollar-a-night budget motel outside Washington. He left the premier and his wife in the car while he went inside and inspected the three adjoining rooms.

"Is this where visiting officials always stay?" the premier asked Remo.

"Only heads of state," Remo said. "We've got a tent in one of the town parks for everybody else."

"Oh," the premier said. "I do not think I would enjoy sleeping in a tent."

Nina asked Remo, "Have you been a friend of Vassily's for a long time?"

"Not really," said Remo. "It's been a short but intense relationship."

"Why is everybody talking to him?" Chiun asked from his rear seat next to Nina. "I am really much more interesting than this thing. If you like, I will tell you about my screenplay."

"What is a screenplay?" asked Nina.

"It is a story for a motion picture," Chiun said. "In your country, they are about tractors and farmers."

"Tell me your story," Nina said.

"You'll be sorry," Remo said.

"Quiet," said Chiun, "or I will write you out of the picture."

"Yes," said the premier. "Tell us this wonderful story."

Chiun was describing the quiet, gentle, peace-loving, handsome, noble, virtuous, and strong main character of the film when Karbenko came back and ushered the premier and his wife into the central of the three motel rooms.

As they unpacked, Chiun was getting around to the fact that this beautiful soul was not appreciated by those around him, particularly those upon whom he had squandered the gift of knowledge only to find them incapable of receiving it.

Karbenko took Remo aside.

"Those were Stantington's men at the airport. I want to go talk to him."

"I'll go with you," Remo said.

"The premier—" Karbenko began.

"He'll be safe," Remo said. "I've heard this screenplay before. It's got four more hours to run. Chiun will never let anything happen to his audience until he's done with the story. We'll be back by then."

"He is very old. Can he protect them?" Karbenko asked.

"If he can't," said Remo, "no one in the world can. Don't write that off as a typical American exaggeration. That's a fact. No one in the world, if he can't."

Chiun had decided that the premier and his wife would probably appreciate the story more if it was told in Russian. He began to tell it in Russian. He started again at the beginning.

Riding up in the elevator toward Stantington's office, Remo asked, "Any ideas on the assassin?"

"None," said Karbenko. "But thank god, he's back in Russia. Let the KGB there find out who he is."

"If they're like our CIA, you're going to have a long wait," Remo said.

"Ain't it the truth, pardner?"

Remo's special director's office pass got them through the guards to Stantington's office complex and the secretary's memory of Remo got them inside Stantington's private office.

"What are you doing here?" Stantington said when he came out of his bathroom. He was staring at Remo.

"He drove me here to make sure I didn't get in an automobile accident," Karbenko said. Stantington glared at him angrily.

"You know that the premier has arrived?" Karbenko said.

Stantington nodded.

"He is staying at the Colony Astor," Karbenko said, naming one of Washington's poshest and oldest hotels. "Can I count on you to assign men there to assist us in protecting him?"

"I have been ordered not to get involved," Stantington said.

"But I'm requesting your help," Karbenko said. "I think that changes the situation."

Stantington sat down behind his desk. "Yes, I suppose it does," he said. "And are you staying at the Colony Astor, too?"

Karbenko nodded. "The premier and his wife are in Room 1902. My men and I are in 1900 and 1904, on both sides of them. I'd like to have some of your men spotted around the hotel, the lobby, the public rooms. Just to watch out for anybody suspicious."

"All right," Stantington said. "I'll have them there in twenty minutes."

"Thank you," Karbenko said. "An unusual thing happened at the airport by the way."

"Oh? What was that?"

"Our car was chased by two carloads of men. Fortunately, they had an accident and we got away."

"Lucky for you," Stantington said.

"Yes, wasn't it? I wonder why they were there?"

Stantington shrugged. "Perhaps they thought the premier was in some danger?"

"Perhaps," Karbenko said. "Thank you for your cooperation, Admiral."

Riding back down in the elevator, Remo asked Karbenko, "Why'd you let him off the hook, if you know those were his guys at the airport?"

"There was no need to push it. I know and he knows I know. I just wanted to be sure what he was up to."

"What is he up to?"

"He thinks I'm the assassin," Karbenko said.

"Are you?"

"If it was me, buddy, he'd be dead by now," the Russian spy said.

"Why'd you give him the song and dance about the Colony Astor Hotel?"

"If he put men out searching for us, they might get lucky and find us," Karbenko said. "This way, he can tie up his men at the other hotel and they won't bother us."

Remo nodded. The Russian colonel was impressive.

"This man is impossible." Nina spat out the words, then wheeled and pointed toward Chiun who sat on the floor, his arms folded under his saffron kimono, looking impassively at the motel wall.

"What happened?" Karbenko asked.

"I wanted to watch television," the premier's wife said. "He told me I should not because all the shows were obscene. If I wanted a good story, he said, he would tell me one. Finally I succeeded in getting the television turned on. I was to watch the news. He told me I should not watch the news. That they were showing pictures of some fat man."

"Yes?" Karbenko said.

"The fat man is the premier. His picture was on the television. Now what do you think of that?"

Karbenko looked at Remo. Remo shrugged.

"Maybe your husband ought to lose some weight," he said.

"Then he broke the knobs off the television set so we could not watch it."

"Philistines," Chiun said. "The Russians were always a people without taste."

"Where is the premier?" Karbenko asked.

"He is in the next room. Watching the television there," Nina said.

"I hope his eyes rot," Chiun said.

"I guess you didn't like Chiun's movie," Remo said.

"We began to get tired of it after the first hour," she said. "So we asked him to stop."

"A Russian could lie in a field of flowers and complain of the smell," Chiun said. "There has not been a sensitive Russian since Ivan the Good."

"Ivan the Good?" Karbenko said. He looked at Remo, a question mark on his face.

"Right," Remo said. "Chiun's family did some work for him once. He paid on time. That raised him from Ivan the Terrible to Ivan the Good."

They left Chiun staring at the wall and went through the open door into the next room.

The premier was sitting on the small single bed, smiling.

"I have been much on your television, American," he told Remo.

"What did they say?" Karbenko asked.

"That I am visiting America to confer with the President about the deaths of our three ambassadors. That our mission here has refused to give any details of my whereabouts or my schedule."

"Good," said Karbenko.

But the premier did not hear the comment. His eyes were fixed, almost glazed, looking at the TV tube.

"Look, Nina. Look," he said, pointing at the tube. "That is where we are going."

Remo and Karbenko leaned over to look.

It was a commercial for Florida's Disneyworld.

Nina nodded.

The premier said. "I want to go there."

"When?" Karbenko said.

"Why not now?"

Karbenko thought for a moment.

"Why not?" he said.

CHAPTER FOURTEEN

At 9 o'clock that night, the premier and his wife, along with Remo, Chiun, Karbenko, and the Russian spy's four top men, were on a private plane heading for Orlando, Florida.

Ten minutes earlier, Admiral Wingate Stantington had learned, in his condominium apartment at Washington's Watergate Complex, that the Russian premier had never checked into the Colony Astor Hotel.

"That son of a bitch," Stantington swore as he slammed down the telephone. Karbenko had done it; he had gotten himself along somewhere with the premier and was just waiting his chance to gun him down.

Not if Stantington could help it though.

Within an hour, his men had found the budget motel where the Earp family had been registered. And only a half hour later, they learned of the specially chartered plane that had left Washington on its way to Orlando.

They checked all the hotels in the Orlando area, before they found one with a block of four rooms registered to Doctor Holliday and family.

Doc Holliday. Karbenko's cowboy passion had given him away.

The hotel manager confirmed that the large group had ordered four taxicabs in the morning to take them to Disneyworld.

Admiral Stantington sat alone in his apartment for an hour, thinking, before he made up his mind.

He would not let Vassily Karbenko assassinate the Russian premier on American soil.

And if there was only one way to stop him, that was the way Stantington would take.

Vassily Karbenko was as good as dead.

CHAPTER FIFTEEN

The premier wanted to go as an American.

"I want to walk the streets and alleys of Disneyworld, like American peoples. I will mingle among them. No one will know we not American."

Karbenko's four KGB agents looked at each other, then they all nodded.

Remo looked at the premier. He was wearing a Hawaiian plaid shirt, and a large straw hat, and big tinted sunglasses as a disguise. But he still had a face like a mudslide and anyone who had seen his picture on television was not likely to mistake him for anyone else.

The four taxicabs arrived on time. Remo, Karbenko, the premier, and Nina crowded into one cab. Two KGB agents rode in the first cab and two more in the third. Chiun insisted on riding alone in the last cab, because he would not share a taxi with Philistines.

"Remember, Chiun," Remo said. "We've got to keep him alive. Nothing else matters."

"Trivia," said Chiun. "All my life is bogged down with trivia."

At the gate, the Russian contingent ran out of

169

money for entrance fees. Disneyworld did not take credit cards, nor did it recognize the International Monetary Fund or Russia's natural gas reserves. This decision was based on the judgment that Russia's natural gas reserves might well run out before Disneyworld did, Disneyworld being an eternal and replenishable resource needing only fresh paint and teenagers who could run around dressed like mice and ducks.

Fortunately, Remo was carrying money and he was able to pay the $2,365.00 in cash for two days of rides for the group. This left the premier with enough money to buy "diplomatic necessities." Everybody got a diplomatic necessity. Karbenko's four KGB men got the winding kind, and the premier and Nina got the digital kind where Mickey Mouse's face appeared and lit up when the diplomatic necessity clicked off noon and midnight. Chiun got one too and proclaimed his love for Russia.

The monorail led over lush green fields with manicured trees. A large perfectly blue lake glistened in the late morning sun. One of the KGB men wondered if they dyed the lake blue.

When they got off the monorail they were greeted by the rich smell of fresh popcorn. To their left was a bank which would translate the cotton crop from Russian Tashkent into American dollars. The Russian cotton crop got the contingent through Snow White and the Seven Dwarfs and Pioneer World.

Chiun wanted a Davy Crockett hat. The premier decided to buy one for everybody, so one of the KGB men was sent back to the Disneyworld bank where he negotiated away mineral rights in the Ukraine, and brought back a satchel of cash to the premier who was waiting at Polynesian World.

The mineral rights also paid for a grass skirt for Nina and Mickey Mouse heads made from coconuts and sea shells.

"This is very nice," Chiun said to Remo, pushing the Davy Crockett tail out of his eyes. "But you are a liar."

"What now?" Remo said.

"Once you took me to a place and told me it was Disneyworld. But that wasn't Disneyworld. This is. You lied to me."

"Chiun, just keep an eye out so that nothing happens to the premier."

By now the Russian party was hungry and the premier found out that the entrance fees did not pay for lunch. Another KGB man was sent back to the main Disneyworld bank, with a promise of two months' tractor production. This allowed everyone to have soft drinks and a meal. When they were done with the meal, no one got up.

Remo asked why they continued to sit at the tables. The premier said the appetizers were a bit flat but he had high hopes for the main course.

When Remo told him he had just eaten the main course, the premier said he would not give up the Balkans for anything, not even a piece of bread.

Finally they settled for foot-long hot dogs, and Disneyworld got the rights to build a Black Sea resort and an option on the Urals.

The Urals did not entitle the Russians to arcade games or dessert.

The premier missed the noon parade of Pluto and Donald Duck and Mickey and Minnie because the contingent was stuck in Future World and could not get over to the main plaza in time. The parade was free, there being no charge for eyesight.

About 1 P.M., Nina confessed that she had the feeling they were looking at the same thing over and over again, with different colored paint.

"There's a trick to telling one exhibit from another," Vassily Karbenko said. "If they have already clipped your ticket book, you've been there, I think."

One of the KGB men on the Paddlewheeler ride wanted to shoot real bullets into the imitation fort to see if anything would happen. Karbenko told him no because he might need his bullets to get out of there if they ran out of money.

Remo said to Chiun, "No sign of any trouble yet."

Chiun looked at his Mickey Mouse wristwatch.

"You have forgotten the lesson of the Great Ung," he said.

"Instantly," Remo agreed.

"Idiot," Chiun said.

Nina wanted a doll from It's a Small Small World, and got one on the premier's promise to conclude a SALT agreement as soon as possible. By now, Nina had a large shopping bag filled with souvenirs.

When they passed the haunted house, there was a sign on the front of the building announcing it was closed for the day.

But a well-tanned young man motioned them to the entrance.

"We've just finished making some improvements inside," he said. "We'd like you to test out the house as our guests. Before we open it to the public."

"You mean free?" the premier asked.

The young man nodded.

"You do not want the Ukraine?"

The man shook his head.

"Our submarine fleet? No cutback in missile construction?" the premier asked suspiciously.

"Free," the young man said.

"Let's go," the premier said. He whispered to Karbenko, "Lenin was right. Given time, the capitalist system will break down."

The heavy door clanged shut behind them as they entered the haunted house. Two of the KGB men led the way as they walked single-file down a long dark corridor.

Remo walked in front of the premier and Nina and Chiun followed them.

Up ahead, there was a faint light at the end of the long dark tunnel, and then they were standing in a large oak-panelled room with oil portraits of men in nineteenth-century garb mounted high up on the walls.

A recorded voice announced that they were going back through time, to another dimension, and as the voice spoke the paintings around the tops of the walls began to change their visage and the men in them seemed to grow younger.

Vassily Karbenko was gone.

CHAPTER SIXTEEN

The electronic voice intoned, "And now, when the secret panel opens, move through the chamber of the past."

There was a faint hissing sound as one of the oaken walls began to slide to the right, revealing another passageway.

Chiun led Nina and the premier through the opening. The four KGB men followed. Remo turned his back and ran back down the dark passageway toward the front entrance.

For ordinary eyes, it would have been almost impossible to see in the corridor. But for Remo, there was no such thing as darkness; there was only less light and more light, and the eye adjusted accordingly. Once all men had seen this way, but now after thousands and thousands of years of laziness, the eye muscle had lost its tone and the eye surfaces their sensitivity, and men had adopted the habit of being blind in the dark. Only a few animals had retained their ability to see at night, and the darkness belonged to them. It belonged to Remo, too.

Flush against one of the wooden panels on the corridor walls, he saw a pushbutton. He pressed it, and the panel hinged back and opened into a small room.

Vassily Karbenko lay on the floor of the room. Blood stained the front of his light blue shirt. His own gun lay in a corner of the room.

Remo knelt over him and Karbenko slowly opened his eyes. He recognized Remo and tried to smile. Blood appeared at the corner of his mouth.

"Hiya, pal," he said.

"Who did it?" Remo asked.

"Stantington's men. That was one of them at the entrance way who let us in," he said. "My own fault. I should have known."

"Don't worry," Remo said. "I'll get help."

"Too late," Karbenko said. "Is the premier all right?"

"He's okay," Remo said. "And I'll keep him that way."

"I know," said Karbenko. He tried to smile again, but the small facial movement caused him pain. His voice came in a slight whisper and his breath in a heavy gasp.

"Sorry I didn't meet you sooner," Remo said. "We could have been a helluva team."

Karbenko shook his head.

"No," he said. "Too many miles between us. If Stantington didn't get me today, it would've been you. You'd have to do it later on 'cause I knew too much about you people."

Remo started to protest, then stopped. Karbenko was right, he realized. He remembered the scene in Smith's office. Smith had told him to protect the premier. He had said that was all . . .

"for now." But later, he would have sent Remo after Karbenko.

"Don't feel bad," Karbenko said. "That's the business we're in." He opened his mouth to speak again but a thick gush of bloody ooze welled up in his mouth. He tried to swallow, could not, and then his head lolled off to the side, his eyes still open, staring at the wall.

Remo stood up. He nodded down at the Russian spy. He felt a curious emotion toward the man, an affection he did not often experience. It was respect and he had thought it no longer lived in him.

"That's the biz, pardner," he said. He turned back to the corridor, to follow the premier, to make sure he was kept alive.

The lights in the chamber of the past had been turned out. But Remo knew where the hidden door was, and he jammed his fingertips like the points of screwdrivers into the wood and yanked it to the left. There was a whooshing sound as his power was pitted against a hydraulic door lock. The whoosh turned into a total expulsion of air from the device and as the air rushed out, the machine's pressure against the door ended, and the oaken panel slammed to the left, crashing into the innards of the door, with a wood-cracking sound.

A twisting corridor stretched out in front of him. Remo went down it at full speed. After twenty yards, the corridor twisted off to the left and opened onto a miniature railroad platform.

Chiun stood on the edge of the platform alone. He looked up as Remo approached.

"Karbenko is dead," Remo said.

Chiun nodded. "He was a good man," he said.

"Where's the premier?"

"He is with the four security men."

Just then a small train appeared at one end of the track and picking up speed, it began to move past them. The four KGB men were on it.

"Where is the premier?" Remo called.

"In the back car," one of the men responded as the train moved quickly past them. The car with the guards vanished into the tunnel. Remo and Chiun looked toward the other end. The last car of the train came by them. The premier and Nina were not on it.

"They must have changed their minds," Remo said.

"Fool," hissed Chiun. He ran to the far end of the platform. A fiberglass wall, molded to look like the stones of a dungeon, separated the train "station" from the small boarding area.

As Remo raced up behind Chiun, he saw the small man leap into the air, and then come down against the wall. His hands flailed out in explosive fury, and the fiberglass splintered and parted, and in the same forward motion, without his feet ever hitting the floor, Chiun was through the rip in the wall. Remo followed him at a dive.

He saw Nina turn toward them. She had been facing her husband over a distance of six feet. When she saw Chiun and Remo she turned again toward her husband. Her finger closed on the trigger of the pistol she held in her hand. But she was too late.

The tiny Oriental, his green kimono swirling

about him, moved in front of her. As the gun fired, he deflected her hand and the bullet dug into the ceiling of the room. Then Chiun had the gun from her hand.

He gave it to Remo.

"Compliments of the Great Ung," he said.

The premier's face was ashen with shock.

"Nina," he said heavily. "You? Why?"

The woman looked at him for a moment, then dropped her head and began to weep. "Because I had to," she sobbed. "I had to."

Remo put his arm around the woman.

"It's okay now. It's all right," he said.

The premier came up to his wife, and took her hands in his. He waited until she lifted her eyes to meet his.

"We go home now, I think," he said.

"Not until I get my ride on the train," Chiun said, inspecting his Mickey Mouse watch.

The President and the premier had met at the White House and issued a joint statement that both condemned all acts of political terrorism and would work jointly to prevent the kind of senseless violence that had cost the lives of three Russian ambassadors in the past week. Project Omega was not mentioned.

Nina met with the President's wife for tea and at a press conference later charmed everyone by announcing how smart and pretty the President's wife was, and that the President's daughter who had spilled a cup of tea on Nina's dress would benefit from a good spanking.

179

The body of Vassily Karbenko, a cultural attache at the Russian embassy in Washington, was found in a lake in Florida. He had been on vacation and apparently had been drowned in a boating accident.

Smith looked across his desk. "I don't understand why," he said.

"MacCleary had gotten close to Nina in the old days," Remo said. "Her husband was barely able to make a living. MacCleary conned her somehow into taking money from him. She needed it to keep the family alive."

"Did he tell her that she'd have to kill her own husband if he became premier?"

"Yes, but she never thought it would happen. Then one day it did and she was stuck."

"Why?" said Smith. "Couldn't she just ignore the Project Omega signal?"

"MacCleary had filled her head full of crap," Remo said. "He had told her that if she didn't act, America would have documents to prove that she was an American spy, and we'd release the documents. This would bring her husband down in disgrace. Probably send both of them to the slave camps. It was better, she figured, for the premier to get killed in America. He'd be regarded then as a glorious Russian hero. She'd rather have her husband a dead patriot than the live husband-of-a-traitor and maybe a traitor himself."

Smith shook his head. "We didn't have any information to release on her. She was safe."

"She didn't know that. MacCleary had really

done a number on her. She didn't say it, but I think they were probably a thing one time. She used to be a good-looking woman," Remo said.

"Well," Smith said, "all's well that ends well."

"You think it ended well?" Remo said.

"Yes. Didn't it?"

"Karbenko died," said Remo. "He was one of them but he was a good man."

"And if the CIA hadn't gotten him, we would have had to," Smith said. "He knew too much."

"That's our rule, right?" said Remo. "Anybody who finds out about CURE is dead meat, right?"

"I wouldn't put it in exactly those terms," Smith said. "But that's about it."

Remo stood up.

"Thank you, Smitty. Have a nice day."

Ruby followed him into the outside office.

"You're strung really tight today," she said. "What's wrong?"

"Karbenko would have had to die because he knew about us," Remo said. "Well somebody else knows about us. And he's still alive."

Ruby shrugged. "Rank has its privileges," she said. "I guess one of them privileges is staying alive."

Remo held her face in his hands and smiled coldly at her.

"Maybe," he said.

It happened just after *Time* magazine's deadline and by the time the next issue came out, the other press had all covered the story to death.

So *Time*'s story was brief:

When Admiral Wingate Stantington, the newly appointed head of the CIA, drowned in the bathtub in his private office bathroom last week, his body was not discovered for a day. CIA personnel had to break into the bathroom by cutting away a lock that had been installed only the week before (at the usual Washington, D.C., cost of $23.65).

Three days later, Ruby yelled at Remo for wasting $23.65 of taxpayers' money and told him if he did it again, she'd give him more trouble than he could handle.

the EXECUTIONER
by Don Pendleton

Over 20 million copies sold!

Mack Bolan considers the entire world a Mafia jungle and himself the final judge, jury, and executioner. He's tough, deadly, and the most wanted man in America. When he's at war, nothing and nobody can stop him.

☐	40-027-9	Executioner's War Book		$1.50
☐	40-299-6	War Against the Mafia	#1	1.50
☐	40-300-3	Death Squad	#2	1.50
☐	40-301-1	Battle Mask	#3	1.50
☐	40-302-X	Miami Massacre	#4	1.50
☐	40-303-8	Continental Contract	#5	1.50
☐	40-304-6	Assault on Soho	#6	1.50
☐	40-305-4	Nightmare in New York	#7	1.50
☐	40-306-2	Chicago Wipeout	#8	1.50
☐	40-307-0	Vegas Vendetta	#9	1.50
☐	40-308-9	Caribbean Kill	#10	1.50
☐	40-309-7	California Hit	#11	1.50
☐	40-310-0	Boston Blitz	#12	1.50
☐	40-311-9	Washington I.O.U.	#13	1.50
☐	40-312-7	San Diego Siege	#14	1.50
☐	40-313-5	Panic in Philly	#15	1.50
☐	40-314-3	Sicilian Slaughter	#16	1.50
☐	40-237-6	Jersey Guns	#17	1.50
☐	40-315-1	Texas Storm	#18	1.50
☐	40-316-X	Detroit Deathwatch	#19	1.50
☐	40-238-4	New Orleans Knockout	#20	1.50
☐	40-317-8	Firebase Seattle	#21	1.50
☐	40-318-6	Hawaiian Hellground	#22	1.50
☐	40-319-4	St. Louis Showdown	#23	1.50
☐	40-239-2	Canadian Crisis	#24	1.50
☐	40-224-4	Colorado Kill-Zone	#25	1.50
☐	40-320-8	Acapulco Rampage	#26	1.50
☐	40-321-6	Dixie Convoy	#27	1.50
☐	40-225-2	Savage Fire	#28	1.50
☐	40-240-6	Command Strike	#29	1.50
☐	40-150-7	Cleveland Pipeline	#30	1.50
☐	40-166-3	Arizona Ambush	#31	1.50
☐	40-252-X	Tennessee Smash	#32	1.50